STORIES FROM THE
ENGLISH AND SCOTTISH
BALLADS

Ruth Manning-Sanders

STORIES FROM THE
ENGLISH AND SCOTTISH
BALLADS

Illustrated by Trevor Ridley

HEINEMANN : LONDON

William Heinemann Ltd

LONDON MELBOURNE TORONTO

CAPE TOWN AUCKLAND

First published 1968

© Ruth Manning-Sanders 1968

Illustrations © William Heinemann Ltd 1968

434 96180 9

Printed in Great Britain by
Western Printing Services Ltd, Bristol

Contents

Introduction   1
The Young Lord of Lorn   5
Hind Horn   17
May Colvin   24
Adam Bell, Clym of the Clough, and
    William of Cloudesley   30
Childe Rowland   44
The Crafty Farmer   52
Tam Lin   56
King Estmere   62
Alison Gross   70
Young Bekie   74
Thomas The Rhymer   82
The Heir of Linne   86
The Lochmaben Harper   93
King Orfeo   97
A Tale of Robin Hood   105

1. The Birth of Robin Hood
2. Robin Hood and Sir Richard at the Lee
3. Sir Richard at the Lee and the Abbot
4. Little John and the Sheriff of Nottingham
5. Robin Hood and the Monk
6. The Sheriff's Shooting Match
7. The Sheriff complains to the King
8. The King and Robin Hood

INTRODUCTION

A BALLAD is a song that tells a story. Nowadays a man or woman who has a story to tell writes it down; it is printed in a book, and those who wish to know the story have only to open the book and read. But there was a time when few of those who had a story to tell, and fewer of those who wished to know the story, could either write or read; and it was then that the ballads were made. For the people of the Middle Ages the ballads took the place of story books, and they were made by the minstrels who roamed the country, singing their stories and accompanying themselves on the harp.

These minstrels were honoured guests everywhere: in the taverns, in the markets, in the cottages, and in the castles of the great lords. In the castle hall, after the supper tables had been removed, the lords and their retainers, the ladies and their maidservants would be all gathered together to listen enthralled to the minstrel's songs that wiled away the tedium of the hours between supper and bed.

The stories that the minstrels sang were on familiar themes. Tender stories of love, stirring stories of well-known battles, of daring raids and captures and rescues, exhilarating stories of heroic resistance and of the doings of bold outlaws, tragic stories of treason and sad deaths, comic stories, cruel and terrible stories, stories of that fairyland in which most men believed—we find them all, sung in direct, vigorous verse to the accompaniment of the minstrel's music.

Sometimes, before the tale is told, there is a little introductory invitation:

I

> Come listen to me, you gallants so free,
> All you that love mirth for to hear,

Or,

> Come all you brave gallants and listen a while,

And then the singer plunges at once into his story, telling it with a rapidity that leaves one almost breathless.

These ballads are dateless and anonymous. Nobody can say when they were invented, or by whom first sung. All we *can* say is that they are very old. The Robin Hood ballads, for instance, were sung throughout the north country at least six hundred years ago, for we find Robin referred to as a hero of popular song by the author of *Piers the Plowman*, a scholar who wrote in the second half of the fourteenth century. But we have no means of telling which King Edward it is that Robin goes to serve, whether Edward I or Edward II.

Robin has his counterpart in the popular heroes of the ballads of other countries; and, in general, we find that most of our English and Scottish ballads tell stories of incidents that occur in the ballad tales of other European nations: of Greece, Germany, Italy, France, Spain and Scandinavia. Nor is this surprising when we remember that during the Middle Ages the telling and hearing of tales was the chief social amusement of all classes of people in all nations of Europe; that the Crusades brought the people of these nations into contact with one another, and that the minstrel was a welcome guest everywhere, a man having no enemies, free to come and go in every country, and to gather his stories—as one might pluck flowers by the wayside—where and how he pleased.

So that the curious reader can, for example, trace in the ballad of King Orfeo and his Isabel the Greek story of Orpheus and Eurydice, transformed by the minstrel singer into a more homely tale adapted to his unlettered audience. But it is perhaps a little surprising to know that a version of another ballad, *Sir Hugh and the Jew's Daughter*, was heard being sung not so very long ago by a group of little coloured children in a street in New York. The children had learned it from an Irish woman, who in her turn had learned it from her mother, whose forbears

2

had carried the memory of tune and words with them across the sea from their old home in Ireland.

And it is entirely due to such 'folk memory' that the ballads exist for us today. With their anonymous authors—the minstrels—long since passed out of existence, and with no contemporary scribe at hand to write them down, the ballads would have sunk into oblivion, were it not that they lived on in the memory of the old country people, who had heard them from their grandparents, and who in turn handed them down to their children and their children's children through many and many a generation. Of course in such handing down many inaccuracies would occur; for memory plays tricks and imagination likes to take a hand, so that we find now a great many variants, both in words and tune, of the same ballad.

For years enough these ballads remained the precious possession of simple country folk only; and then suddenly scholars woke up to the fact of what treasures we were in danger of losing, and began to collect and edit them. The first man to do so was Bishop Percy, who published his *Reliques of Ancient English Poetry* in 1765. Percy was followed by Sir Walter Scott in his *Minstrelsy of the Scottish Border*, and by many others: most notably by Professor E. J. Child, whose splended and exhaustive collection, *The English and Scottish Popular Ballads*, was published at the close of the nineteenth century.

Of all the ballads now left to us those that come from the north country and the borderland between England and Scotland are the finest: perhaps because in that remote district the country folk retained the memory of their minstrel heritage longer than they did in places that were nearer to centres of learning. Be that as it may, these particular ballads have been truly described as 'the richest body of popular poetry in the world'.

And finally it must be said how much is lost in the telling of these stories in prose. They were born in song, and their lyric quality is their greatest charm. Told in swift, vivid verse that leaps from happening to happening and never dallies over detail, leaving much to the imagination, and with the author counting for nothing, they carry us along like a river in full

3

spate. In their manner of telling and in their emotional appeal they are unique—there is nothing else like them in the whole realm of poetry.

But, as the ballads have been collected and set down in the dialect of the people who sang them, they are not, in their verse form, easy for children to read. Some of them indeed, are very difficult. And so we are now giving you these stories told in prose; in the hope that, coming to know them and like them in this form, you may later on be led to read them for yourself in the original verse. You will find them gathered together in *The Oxford Book of Ballads* (Quiller Couch), and in my own collection *A Bundle of Ballads* (also published by the Oxford University Press).

4

THE YOUNG LORD OF LORN

THE LORD OF LORN had one little son, and he sent him away to school. The little boy was very clever; he learned more in one day than any of the other children could learn in three; and when he had been at the school for some time, the schoolmaster said, 'My little lord, I think it's time you got you home again, for truly I can teach you nothing more.'

So the little boy's horse, bitted and bridled with gold, was brought round; the little boy said goodbye to his schoolfellows and rode home to his parents.

And when he came to them, he knelt before them.

And his mother, the Lady of Lorn, raised him up and kissed him. And his father, the Lord of Lorn, said, 'Why, my little son, what tidings have you brought that you come home to us so soon?'

'Good tidings, I hope, my father,' said the little boy. 'There is not a book in all Scotland that I have not read, and my master can teach me nothing more.'

Then the Lord of Lorn rejoiced. 'Well done, my little son!' said he. 'Now we will send you into France, that you may learn courtly manners, and to speak the language. This very day I will write a letter to the Duke of France, that he may take you into his household.'

So the letter was written and sent. And in due time an answer came: the Duke of France would receive the Lord of Lorn's young son and care for him tenderly.

'But who shall we send with our little son to be his guide and counsellor?' said the Lady of Lorn. 'For the child is too young to go alone among strangers.'

'We will send our head steward to go with him,' said the Lord of Lorn. 'For he is a true man.'

So they summoned the head steward and told him. And the steward swore an oath that he would watch over the little boy with all truth and honour.

Then the Lady of Lorn gave the steward a thousand pounds. 'Steward,' said she, 'be but true to our little son, and when you come back I will give you much more.'

And the steward said, 'If I be not true to him, and to you my lord and lady, may I be burned at the stake!'

So the Lady of Lorn dressed her little son in fine garments: a velvet gown, a satin doublet, crimson hose, shoes of Spanish leather with gold buckles, and a velvet hat with a curling ostrich feather. She hung a gold chain round his neck, put jewelled rings on his fingers, and a jewelled brooch at his collar; and when they came to part, she embraced him and wept over him and said, 'Little son, wherever you go, my heart goes with you.'

The Lord of Lorn wept, the little boy wept, the servants wept and crowded round the little boy to wish him well. And the steward put his handkerchief to his eyes and turned his head aside, as if he, too, were overcome at this tender parting. But behind his handkerchief the steward was smiling an evil smile, for he was false, false at heart.

So the little boy and the steward went on shipboard, and the Lord and Lady of Lorn, with a crowd of attendants, stood on the quay to watch the gallant ship set sail. As long as the ship was in sight they stood on the quay and waved to their little son, and he took off his velvet hat and waved back to his dear parents.

And the steward said to the ship's captain, 'What an affecting sight, truly it melts my heart! But my little lord is safe enough with me.'

'I do not doubt it,' said the good captain. 'But if I did doubt it sir steward, by heaven I would take you up in my two arms and cast you overboard!'

All went merrily and well until the ship reached the French coast. And there the little boy and the steward went ashore amid the cheers and good wishes of all the crew. The steward and the little boy set off on two fine horses to travel to the castle of

6

the Duke of France, and the ship sailed back to Scotland.

Alack! Alack! No sooner was the ship gone out of sight, than the steward began to treat the little boy most shamefully. He made the child ride behind him, he taunted and mocked him, he refused to give him any food, or any money to buy food; and the little boy grew hungrier and thirstier and more and more miserable.

So one day, when they were dismounted and resting by the roadside, the steward took a flagon of wine from his saddle bag and set it to his false lips; and the little boy said, 'Oh cruel steward, give me one drink of the wine, I pray you, or I must die of thirst!'

And the steward answered, 'If you thirst, go drink of the pond yonder. Water is good enough for you!'

So the little boy ran to the pond and knelt to cup the water in his hands. And the steward came quickly behind him and pushed him into the pond. 'Now you may drown!' said he. 'For I won't be burdened with you one moment longer!'

And every time the little boy struggled to gain the bank, the steward pushed him deeper into the water.

'Steward! Steward!' gasped the little boy. 'Only spare my life and I will give you all that I am heir to!'

'Is that a promise?' said the steward. 'Or will you break your word?'

'I have never broken my word in my life,' cried the little boy, 'nor will I now!'

So then the steward dragged him out of the pond and set him roughly on his feet. 'Now,' said he, 'remember you have given me your word. You are no longer Heir of Lorn: that title belongs to me.'

'Then who am I?' said the little boy. 'And what is my name?'

'*Your* name! Let me see! Yes, your name is Poor Disaware, and you shall go hire you to a shepherd to tend his flocks. But if you breathe one word of what has happened here to any man living, remember that word shall be your last. I must have your oath on that again.'

And the little boy said, 'I swear to you, steward, I will not breathe a word to any man living of what has happened here.'

7

'Nor to no woman either?' said the steward.

'Nor to no woman neither,' said the little boy.

'Then Poor Disaware,' said the steward, 'take off that velvet gown, for a shepherd boy does not go fine.'

The little boy took off his velvet gown.

'Now take off your crimson hose and your fine Spanish leather shoes with the gold buckles.'

So the little boy took off his hose and his shoes.

'And now off with that gold chain about your neck, the jewelled rings on your fingers, and the jewelled brooch at your neck; and off with your satin doublet, and your silk shirt embroidered with gold.'

The little boy took off all these things: and there he stood, stark naked.

'Hey, hey!' mocked the steward, as he gathered up the little boy's clothes, 'I see Poor Disaware's skin is white as any lily flower! A princess might well fall in love with that white skin, my lad! So we must haste to cover it up! Here!' And he fetched from his baggage a rough coat of undyed wool, and long hose to match. Yes, that crafty steward had brought those clothes with him for this very purpose!

'Cover up your tender skin with these, Poor Disaware!' said he.

So the little boy put on the rough wool coat and the coarse hose.

'Now, be off with you, out of my sight!' said the steward.

And the little boy ran off sobbing.

He ran till he was out of breath, and then he sat down in a wood to rest, and then he got up and ran again, not knowing where he was going. And all the time he was sobbing.

And by and by he came to a wide grassy place where sheep were grazing, and on one side of the wide grassy place was a shepherd's hut. And the shepherd stood at the door.

So the little boy went up to the shepherd and said, 'Do you want a servant lad to tend your sheep?'

'That I do!' said the shepherd. 'For I have no child of my own. And you have a pretty face, my boy, and a sweet voice, though you speak our tongue but awkwardly.'

8

'That is because I was born in Scotland, sir.'

'And where are those who should be looking after you?' said the shepherd.

'Oh sir!' cried the little boy, 'I am deserted by all!' And he began to sob again.

The shepherd took the child in to his wife, and she fed and comforted him. But to all their questions he would answer nothing, except that he was Poor Disaware, and that he was alone in the world.

But they loved him and cared for him. So there we may leave him for a while, helping to tend the sheep. For we must see what the false steward is doing.

Well, the steward rode on till he came to a town, and there he sold the little boy's clothes, and the little boy's rings that were too small for his fat fingers. But he kept the gold chain, and the jewelled brooch to deck himself with. And with the money he got for the clothes and the rings he bought himself a suit that any lord might have envied. He could well fling money about, for he had also the thousand pounds that the Lady of Lorn had given him. And he had all the people in the town bowing and scraping to him, you may be sure.

So, when he had lived in that town for a while, vaunting himself as the Heir of Lorn, he hired a page to ride behind him, and himself proudly astride the horse with the gold bit and bridle, off he set in grand style till he came to the castle of the Duke of France. There he announced himself as the Heir of Lorn, and was welcomed by the good Duke, though perhaps the Duke was a little surprised to find the Heir of Lorn older than he had been led to expect.

Now the Duke had a beautiful little daughter, and he thought, 'What better match for my girl than the rich Heir of Lorn?' So he spoke to the false heir about it.

'When my daughter is a wedded wife,' said he, 'I will give her husband a thousand pounds a year. And if you are willing, I would like that husband to be you. Of course she is too young to marry yet, but I like to get these things arranged, and she is not too young to be betrothed.'

And the false Heir of Lorn creased up his face into a gracious smile, and said nothing would please him better.

The Duke of France didn't think of asking his little daughter what *she* thought about it; for a girl in those days must do as her father bid her. Only she asked that the betrothal might be put off for a time. 'For,' said she, 'I would like to play and make merry for a little while longer, and to be betrothed will make me feel quite grown up.' And she looked shyly at the false Heir of Lorn, and then turned away her head. No, she didn't like him; she didn't like him one little scrap, that was the truth of it.

'Silly girl!' said the Duke of France. 'But I suppose we must humour her, eh, my Lord of Lorn?'

And the false steward said, 'Oh yes, yes certainly.' But he wasn't too well pleased.

So one day the Duke's young daughter rode out with her pages and her maidens, and came to the place where the poor little Heir of Lorn sat watching the sheep. And he was sighing and moaning to himself.

'Oh if my father did but know, oh if my lady mother did but know what has become of me!'

And the Duke's young daughter heard his moans and said to one of her maidens, 'Go, bid that shepherd boy come to me. I would know what grieves him.'

So the maiden went to the little Lord of Lorn and said, 'Boy, you must come to my lady.'

And the boy went and knelt down before her—*he* hadn't to learn how to behave in a lady's presence!

Said she, 'What is your name? Where were you born? And why do you sigh and moan?'

Said he, 'I am Poor Disaware, my lady. I was born in Scotland. And I sigh and moan for one who died—oh long ago!'

'From Scotland!' said she. 'Then tell me, bonny boy, do you know of the young Heir of Lorn? For he is come into France to woo me.'

'Yes, my lady,' answered he. 'I know that young lord right well. And I swear to you he is upright and true—and oh were he but back in his own country!'

'And what mean you by that?' said she.

'Nothing, my lady,' said he, 'except that home is best.'

The Duke's young daughter looked at him. No she didn't turn away her head. She smiled and looked into his eyes, and smiled and looked. She thought he had the nicest face of any lad she had ever seen. 'Will you leave your sheep,' she said, 'and come and be my page?'

'Yes, my lady, if the shepherd will agree,' he said. For indeed he thought he had never met with a lovelier or kinder little maiden.

So he ran to ask the shepherd, and the shepherd said, 'Go, my lad, for I think your courtly manners suit better the life of a page than the life of a rough shepherd's boy.'

So now we have the little Heir of Lorn dressed in fine clothes and waiting on the Duke's young daughter, and knowing just how to carry himself, you may be sure. And in everything he did, he pleased her more and more.

But when the false steward saw him he stamped with rage. 'You vagabond!' he cried. 'How dare you come here masquerading in front of my betrothed, and giving yourself airs? You are a vile thief, and you know it!'

But the Duke's young daughter tossed her head and frowned. 'Have done, my Lord of Lorn,' said she to the steward. 'He is *my* page, and you must show him good will, or you'll get no favour from me!'

So the false steward hurried off to the Duke. 'Do you know whom your daughter has taken into her service now?' he said. 'A scurvy little rascal from Scotland, whose father, believe it or not, robbed *my* father of thirty thousand pounds. Yes, and was hanged from over the castle wall for that theft, to be sure!'

The Duke sent for the page boy and said, 'Tell me the truth, who are you?'

'I am Poor Disaware from Scotland,' said the page.

'And did your father steal from my Lord of Lorn's father?' said the Duke.

'Oh, how could he, how could he?' cried the poor boy. And he burst into tears.

Now no one could look on the poor young Heir of Lorn's face without loving him, and the Duke's heart was stirred with pity for his sad lot. 'I cannot let you be my daughter's page,' said he, 'for only those of noble birth should attend her. But tell me, do you love horses?'

'Yes, I love them well,' said the boy.

'Then get you to the stables, and I will give you employment there,' said the Duke.

And so it was arranged, and the false steward had to grin and bear it, though he would rather have seen the boy hanged.

The young Heir of Lorn worked in the Duke's stables for several years and grew into a fine strapping lad. And so gentle and courteous was he that all the men of the Duke's household became his friends.

The Duke's little daughter was growing, too, into a graceful young girl. But she kept putting off the day of her betrothal with one excuse or another. She didn't love the false steward any the better for having robbed her of her favourite page! And often when she was out with her maidens, she would visit the stables that she might see her former page at work.

Now one day, when she was in the garden, she saw this former page of hers leading a colt to water in the brook that ran at the bottom of the garden. And the colt, who was fresh and frisky, having taken a long drink, suddenly tossed up his head and hit the young Heir of Lorn in the eye.

And the young Heir of Lorn started back and cried, 'Oh you wicked colt! Do you know what you have done? You have struck a lord of high degree! But there, I suppose I must forgive you, my poor colt, for how can you tell a lord from a loon when rigged out in stable clothes? Oh me, if I could but let my father know how basely I have been served.'

13

And when the Duke's young daughter heard that, she left her maidens in the garden and ran down to the brook.

'Stable boy, stable boy,' she cried, '*who* are you? There is some mystery here that I cannot understand! But tell me, tell me, only tell me the truth and I will help you!'

And he answered, 'My lady, I cannot tell you. I have sworn an oath that I will tell no man or woman living, and I will not break my oath.'

'Then tell your tale to the colt,' said she. 'Tell it all out clear and plain in the colt's ear; and so you may save your oath.'

So the young Heir of Lorn put his arm about the colt's neck, and told out all his sad tale from the beginning into the colt's ear. And the Duke's daughter listened. And when the tale was told, she went to her father.

'Father,' said she, 'I have often asked you to put off the day of my betrothal, and you have been kind and humoured me. So now, if you will but put it off for three months longer, I will do all that you desire of me.'

'Well, well, you are a foolish wench,' said the Duke of France. 'But yes, you shall have your way.'

Truth to tell, the more the Duke saw of the false steward, the less he liked him; and he was beginning to doubt in his own mind whether the match would really be a good thing.

The Duke's daughter made him a graceful curtsy, and hurried away to write a letter to the Lord of Lorn in Scotland. She told him all the sad tale that the young Heir of Lorn had told to the colt, and the letter came safely into the Lord of Lorn's hand. Oh, how the Lady of Lorn wept when she heard how her son had been treated! But the old Lord of Lorn said, 'Peace, peace, my lady! This is no time for tears, it is a time for vengeance!'

And he called up five hundred of his knights and men-at-arms, chartered a ship, and set sail for France. The wind was fair, the voyage speedy—Lord of Lorn, knights, men-at-arms, horses and all, they soon landed in France. And set off with all haste for the Duke's castle.

And when they came to the green outside the castle gates, who should they see, exercising the Duke's charger there on the green, but the young Heir of Lorn.

Then there came such a ringing cheer as set the castle walls echoing. The knights threw their hats in the air, the men-at-arms went down on their knees. And the false steward looked from a window and said, 'What fools are they out there? Have they all gone mad that they pay a mere stable boy such courtesy?'

Then the old Lord of Lorn raised his voice in a great shout. 'False thief and traitor, you shall not escape my vengeance for what you have done!'

And he bade his men surround the castle on all sides, and then he went in and told the whole truth to the Duke of France.

There was no escape for the false steward. He hid in a cupboard, but the Duke's men dragged him out, and brought him before the Lord of Lorn. And the Lord of Lorn said, 'False steward, what were the words you said to the Lady of Lorn and myself when we bid you be true to our little son?'

The false steward, whose teeth were chattering with fright, protested that he had said nothing. So the Lord of Lorn repeated the words for him: 'If I be not true to him, and to you, my lord and lady, may I be burned at the stake.'

'You have pronounced your own doom,' said the Lord of Lorn.

But the Heir of Lorn cried out, 'Oh my father, that is too cruel a death!'

So they beat the false steward with rods and turned him out to wander whither he willed. And what became of him none knew nor cared. And the Duke of France said:

'My Lord of Lorn, we have been spared the most wicked betrothal that ever was known. And I would that we might now have, instead of a betrothal, a merry wedding. For if I am not mistaken we have a pair of lovers here. And though they are young, they are not too young. What say you, my daughter, will you take the Heir of Lorn for your husband?'

And the Duke's daughter smiled and curtsied and said, 'I will do as my father wishes.'

'And what say you, young Heir of Lorn, will you take my daughter and a gift of a thousand pounds a year?'

And the young Heir of Lorn laughed and said, 'I would

rather have her with a ring of gold than all the wealth you can offer me!'

So they held a merry wedding. And after it was over, the Lord of Lorn, and the young Heir of Lorn and his bride, and the five hundred Scottish knights and men-at-arms sailed back to Scotland. And there they lived in peace and happiness for many, many years.

HIND HORN

Hind Horn fair, and Hind Horn free,
With a hey lillelu and a how lo lan;
Where were you born, in what countrie?
And the birk and the broom blows bonnie.

WELL, Hind Horn says he was born in the greenwood, and left
there all forlorn. But he was a handsome lad, and a gallant one,
and when he was no more than a stripling, not yet grown to
manhood, he went to serve the king of Scotland. And when he
saw the king's lovely little daughter, Jean, his heart went out to
her: it seemed to him that there was nothing in all the world so
precious and beautiful as that young girl. And every day he
thought of her more and more.

And when young Jean found this handsome lad so attentive to
her wishes, and always ready to do anything, small or great, that
would please her—why then every day young Jean thought of
him more and more. Yes, she came to love him, and he loved her;
and so it went on for seven years, with the two of them growing
up to manhood and womanhood, and loving each other more
and more with every year that passed.

Until they met among the rose bushes in the king's garden,
when none was by. And there they told of their love, and
plighted their troth.

But the king had quite other ideas for his beautiful daughter;
she was to marry a prince, no less. And when she told him that
it was Hind Horn she would marry and none other, the king
sent for Hind Horn and bid him begone out of the country, and
never return if he wished to keep his head on his shoulders.

Before he went, Hind Horn managed to see Jean just once

more. It was in the rose garden again that they met, when the sun had gone down and the first stars were dimly shining. And after they had kissed each other again and again, and sworn to be true for ever and ever, princess Jean gave Hind Horn a gold ring, set with seven bright diamonds.

Said she, 'As long as these diamonds keep their hue, you will know that I am happy and true to you. But should they lose their sparkle and turn pale, then, oh my love, you'll know that all is over between us. It will not mean that I love another man, for that I can never do; but it will mean that I am forced to wed another against my will.'

And so they bade each other goodbye, and Hind Horn crossed the sea, and took service with the king of Ireland. There he did many valiant deeds, and rose to such favour that the Irish king loaded him with honours and riches, made him a lord, and offered him his daughter in marriage. But Hind Horn remained faithful to his dear love, Princess Jean. Every day he looked at his ring, and still the diamonds glowed and sparkled; and he sighed and smiled and said to himself, 'My love is happy and true to me.'

But there came a morning when looking on his ring he saw that the diamonds sparkled no longer. He stared at them in horror: they stared back at him as dull and dead-seeming as the eyes of dead fishes.

What to do? Hind Horn didn't think twice; he ran to the Irish king and told him he must go back to Scotland. And he took ship and went. And with him on board went a good grey steed that the Irish king gave him.

And as soon as he landed on Scottish soil, he set off riding to the king's court: lose his head or keep his head, see Princess Jean he must and would. And if she were wedded to another, why then he would as soon lose his head as keep it.

So, after a hard gallop, as he was nearing the king's castle, he came to a spring, and lighted down that his horse might drink. And he saw, leaning on a staff and hobbling towards him, an old beggar man, wearing a dirty brown hood and a tattered cloak.

'Alms, alms, good sir!' whined the old man, holding out his begging bowl.

Hind Horn flung a coin into the bowl and said, 'What news, what news in this country, old man? For it's seven long years that I've been away.'

'No news at all, that I know of,' said the beggar man. 'Save that there's a wedding at the king's court. The strangest wedding ever you heard of! The wedding feast has been going on for forty-two days, because the bride is peevish and won't take her man.'

Says Hind Horn, 'If you will give me your tattered old cloak, you shall have my good grey steed.'

Says the old beggar, all astonished, 'But sir, my tattered cloak is not for you; your good grey steed is not for me!'

Says Hind Horn, 'Will you give me your old brown hood? And I will give you my gold-laced hat.'

Says the old beggar, 'But sir, your gold-laced hat is not for the likes of me! And my dirty brown hood is not for the likes of you!'

Says Hind Horn, 'If you will give me your staff and your begging bowl, you shall have my scarlet cloak.'

'But sir, but sir, your scarlet cloak is not for the likes of me; my begging bowl and staff are not for the likes of you!'

But Hind Horn wouldn't be denied. They changed clothes: the beggar man, in scarlet cloak and wearing the gold-laced hat, rode off on the good grey steed. And Hind Horn, with the dirty brown hood wrapped close round his face, and the tattered cloak covering his gold-embroidered jerkin, hobbled off with staff and begging bowl to the king's castle.

And there at the castle gate he stood, mumbling and grimacing, till the porter asked him what he wanted.

Says Hind Horn, 'I hear it is the custom in this country, when the wedding feast is held, for the bride to bring a cup of wine in her own fair hands to any who may ask it. Go, tell the bride there is a beggar at the gate who asks a cup of wine for Hind Horn's sake.'

So the porter went in with the message. Princess Jean was sitting at the feast. She wore a crown of gold, and her wedding dress shimmered with pearls and diamonds. But if ever a bride looked miserable, that bride was Princess Jean. Her face was

19

deadly white, and tears kept rising in her eyes. But when she heard the name of Hind Horn, she jumped up from the table, filled a gold cup with wine, and down the stairs with her and out across the court to the castle gate, as fast as any hare.

'What news, what news, you old beggar man?'

'No news at all, you bonny bride. I did but ask a cup of wine in the name of him whom once you loved.'

He drank up the wine, dropped his ring into the cup, and handed the cup back to princess Jean.

And when Princess Jean saw the ring, she cried out, 'Oh where, where did you get it? Did you get it by sea, did you get it by land, or did you take it off a dead man's finger?'

'I did not get it by sea or land, my lady. I did not take it off a dead man's finger. And where I got it, you should know, for I got it from your very own hand.'

Then he raised his head and flung back his dirty brown hood, and she knew him.

'Oh,' said she, 'I'll cast off my wedding dress and follow you from town to town. I'll throw away my golden crown and beg

21

with you to win our bread. I'll fling away my rings and all my jewels and follow you forever more!'

And Hind Horn turned and walked away, and she followed him. But at a little distance from the castle gate, he stopped and laughed.

'No need, my Jean, to cast away your crown, for I can make you lady of many a rich province. No need for you to fling down your gold and your jewels, for I can add gold to gold and jewels to jewels. No need to cast off your wedding dress, for this shall be our wedding day.'

And he threw off his dirty brown hood and his beggar's cloak, and there he stood—a very prince to look at, with his jerkin embroidered in gold, and his collar studded with pearls. So off they went and got married. And since what was done couldn't be undone, the king of Scotland had to make the best of it.

The bridegroom thought the bride for to wed,
With a hey lillelu and a how lo lan;
But young Hind Horn has got her instead,
And the birk and the broom blows bonnie.

MAY COLVIN

MAY COLVIN was a very beautiful girl. She was also a very spoilt girl, who thought she could do as she pleased about everything. And as she was an only child, whose mother was dead, and whose father was very rich and doted on her, she did do as she pleased about most things.

Of course among the guests who came to her father's castle, there were many young men who came to woo May Colvin. But no, she wouldn't have any of them! She had some fault to find with them all: one was too old, one was too young, one was too silly, one was too ugly, one was too masterful—she laughed with them, she teased them, she egged them on, she held them off, until they got weary of wooing her and went away.

And then came false Sir John. Now false Sir John was not the kind of man who would take no for an answer. He was also not the kind of man that May Colvin's father, spoil her as he might, would have dreamed of letting her marry; and perhaps that made the naughty, wayward girl all the more inclined to favour him. True, she flirted with him for a long time; one day all smiles and sweetness, the next day all stand-offish and snubbing. But false Sir John took no notice of her uppish ways; wherever she went, indoors or out, in the gardens, in the hall, in this room or that—there was Sir John coaxing and whispering his love into her ears. Oh yes, false Sir John was after a good thing, and he meant to have it!

'But my father wouldn't let me marry you!' pouted May Colvin, when Sir John had asked her for the hundredth time to be his wife.

'We can do without his permission,' whispered Sir John. 'We might run away together—eh, my lovely one?'

'But then I should come to you without a penny,' laughed May Colvin.

'Oh no, my precious, oh no!' whispered false Sir John. 'Your father has coffers crammed full with gold, and I think you know where the keys are? Your father has a stable full of magnificent horses, and the bolt of the stable door could easily be drawn back by your little hand. . . . And then away with us into the north country to get married before anyone could stop us.'

To run off with bags full of gold and the two best horses in her father's stable! That would be an adventure indeed! And the more May Colvin thought about it, the more the idea of such an adventure excited her. As to her fond father, May Colvin didn't trouble her head much about what *he* would do or say: once she was married he would have to put up with it. And of course he would forgive her!

So one night, when all the castle slept, May Colvin tripped downstairs, unlocked the door of her father's treasury (oh yes, the cunning young monkey had well oiled the key and it turned without a sound) unlocked the great iron coffers that stood there, stuffed into two bags as much money as they would hold —gold money, that is, for the silver she left untouched—tiptoed with the bags out into the castle court, where false Sir John was waiting in the shadows, handed the money bags to Sir John, and tripped off to the stables, with him at her heels.

Which horses should it be—this one, that one?

'The fastest, the strongest, and the best,' whispered false Sir John.

'Then the milk-white steed for me, and the big dapple grey for you,' said May Colvin.

And in less than no time the horses were saddled, bridled, and led out; and the two of them mounted and off.

Away and away and away: the night wind in their faces, the clouds racing over the moon above them. What fun it was! May Colvin laughed and sang: she had never done anything like this before, and she wouldn't have missed doing it for the world! Not a thought did she give to the kind of man she was running away with. But she was soon to find out.

The country they were galloping through grew wilder and wilder, and more and more desolate. And at last they came to a lonely sea shore. And there, by a rock that overhung the water, false Sir John pulled up his dapple grey, and seized the milk-white steed by the bridle.

May Colvin suddenly felt frightened.

'Why are we stopping here?' she asked. And though she tried to show no fear, her voice trembled.

The moon shone out from behind a cloud: it shone on Sir John's face, and no devil from hell could have looked uglier. 'Why are we stopping here?' said he. 'We are stopping here because it is journey's end.' And he gave a fiendish laugh. 'Get off your horse! I have drowned seven gay ladies here, and you shall be the eighth. Get off that horse, I say; for I don't intend that *he* shall drown!'

And May Colvin got off her horse, and stood helplessly on the rock.

False Sir John also dismounted. There he was, close beside her, and looking her up and down.

'Now,' says he, 'take off your silken robes and lay them on the rock. For they are too fine and costly to rot in the sea along with you.'

And May Colvin took off her silk dress and her embroidered petticoat, and laid them on the rock. There she stood now, in her linen chemise and her stays.

'Take off your satin stays,' said Sir John. 'Take off your gold-buckled shoes and your fancy stockings. For they are too fine and costly to rot in the sea, along with you.'

And May Colvin took off her satin stays and her gold-buckled shoes and her stockings, and laid them on the rock. And though she was terribly frightened, she was angry too. A great rage came over her that *she*, May Colvin, she, her father's darling, she, whose merest whim had always been law, was now about to be thrown into the sea, and drowned like an unwanted kitten! So when false Sir John bade her take off her chemise, for he meant to have that too, she said:

27

'Turn your back on me then, false Sir John, look up at the moon and the clouds. For it never became a gentleman to look on a naked lady.'

False Sir John laughed, he turned his back, he looked up at the moon and the clouds: May Colvin flung her arms about his waist, and pushed him off the rock into the sea.

Down he went, up he came, splashing and spluttering.

'Oh, reach me your hand, May Colvin, or else I drown! I'll take you home to your father's castle, I swear—'

'I can get back without you, false Sir John,' said May Colvin.

And she put on her satin stays and her stockings and her gold-buckled shoes.

Down went Sir John again, up he came once more, splashing and spluttering. 'Help! Help!' he cried, 'for pity's sake!'

'No help, no help, false Sir John,' answered May Colvin. 'No help, and no pity. You will not lie in a colder bed than the one you had planned for me.'

And she put on her embroidered petticoat and her silk dress. Down went Sir John again. But this time he did not rise.

May Colvin jumped onto the milk-white steed, took the dapple grey by the rein, and away with her at full gallop.

All through the rest of the night she rode, and reached her father's gate an hour before the dawn. She put the two horses back in the stable; and then she tiptoed into the castle, carrying the two bags of gold. She stole to her father's treasury, emptied the gold into one of the iron coffers, and tucked the two empty bags under her arm. Then up the stairs she crept, a thoroughly subdued and trembling maiden, praying that she might get to her room unseen of anyone.

But at the head of the stairs was her parrot, waltzing round the bars of his cage, and looking at her with his head cocked to one side.

And the parrot up and spoke.

'May Colvin, *where* have you been? And what have you done with that false Sir John who went with you last night?'

'Hush, hush, my pretty parrot, oh hush my pretty bird!' whispered May Colvin. 'I entreat you to tell no tales of me! If

28

you'll but hold your tongue, I'll give you a cage of beaten gold and a perch of ivory!'

So the parrot didn't say another word. He just blinked his bright little eyes and looked very, very knowing.

May Colvin ran to her room. Now she was safe!

But no! Her father was awake, and he had heard the parrot speaking. So he opened his bedroom door and looked out.

'What is the matter with the pretty parrot,' said he, 'that it prattles like this an hour before daylight?'

The parrot swung himself upside down. He worked himself swiftly round his cage, clinging to the bars, now with his beak, now with his claws. His little eyes were fairly sparkling with amusement.

'Nothing ails me *now*, master,' said he, 'nothing at all! But a cat came prowling round my cage, and I thought it would have worried me. So I just called out to May Colvin to drive the cat away.'

'And did May Colvin get rid of the cat for you, my pretty bird?'

'Oh yes she did, master. The cat won't come again.'

So May Colvin's father went back into his room and shut the door. And May Colvin jumped into her bed, pulled the clothes up round her head, and laughed and cried.

ADAM BELL, CLYM OF THE CLOUGH, AND WILLIAM OF CLOUDESLEY

ADAM BELL and Clym of the Clough and William of Cloudesley were three bold yeomen of the north country, and they were outlawed for shooting the king's deer. So they fled to Inglewood Forest, near merry Carlisle: and there they went on shooting the king's deer, and lived without a care. At least, Adam Bell and Clym of the Clough lived without a care, for they were not married; but William of Cloudesley had a wife and three little sons in Carlisle, and sometimes there came over him a great longing to see them again.

So one night he made up his mind that he *would* see them, and he said to his comrades, 'Brothers, I'm away to Carlisle to see how it fares with Alice, my wife, and my three little sons.'

'Then you don't go by *my* counsel!' said Adam Bell. 'Just stop and think, brother! If the Justice catches you, as sure as I'm alive, you'll be dangling at a rope's end by morning!'

But William was determined to go. Nothing would stop him.

'If I'm not back by six o'clock tomorrow morning,' says he, 'why then you'll know that I've either been killed or taken prisoner.'

And off he went, despite all that the other two could say.

It was a dark night, and he got into Carlisle without being seen. He crept stealthily from street to street till he reached his own house. And there he tapped on the window.

'Alice, Alice,' whispered he; 'it's your husband, William of Cloudesley! Open and let me in!'

Alice hurried to open the door. She was in his arms next minute. But what was she saying? 'Oh William, William, you shouldn't have come! Don't you know that the Justice has set a watch on this house? He's been waiting to catch you this half year or more!'

William drew the bolt across the door, and laughed. 'But now I'm here, dear wife,' said he, 'let us eat and drink and make merry.'

Alice, like the devoted wife she was, bustled off into her larder and fetched out the best of all she had. And William's three little sons scrambled shouting from their beds to hug and kiss him. And when Alice had set the table, they all sat down to eat.

Now in a corner by the fire sat an old, old woman, whom William had long ago taken into his house out of charity. For seven years she had been fed and clothed by Alice and William, and in all that time she had never been out of the house, or moved more than a step or two from her corner by the fire, for she was lame, and made out to be lamer than she was, lest she be put to help about the house. Alice now served the old woman with meat and drink, and there she sat, mumbling and muttering to herself. But when her plate was empty, and Alice and William were talking together and taking no notice of her— what did she do? Up she got—the devil fly away with her!— crept stealthily out of the house, and off with her to the Justice.

There she stands now before the Justice, grinning all over her ugly old face.

'Ha, ha!' says she, and 'Ho, ho!' says she. 'This night is come to town one it would make you merry to have between your hands!'

Says the Justice, 'And who's that, old woman?'

Says she, 'Who but William of Cloudesley?'

Was the Justice merry? Was he not! He called the sheriff, and the sheriff hurried off to summon a band of armed men.

'Old woman, old woman,' said the Justice, 'you shan't have travelled here for nothing! You shall have your reward before you go!'

And he gave her a fine new gown of scarlet cloth.

The old woman took the gown, hobbled back home, and sat

31

her down again in her corner by the fire. And William and Alice, having other things to think about, took no notice either of her going out, or of her coming back.

But what was this? William lifted his head to listen: yes, out in the street, the babble of many voices, the tramp of many feet! Alice ran to the window and looked out. What did she see? The Justice and the sheriff with a great crowd of armed men, and the men were surrounding the house.

'Alas! Alas! Treason! Treason!' she cried. 'Go into my chamber, dear William, for that is the strongest room in the house!'

William picked up his sword and his buckler, his bow and arrows, called his three children to come with him, and ran into Alice's chamber. Alice, like a true wife, snatched up a pole axe and went to stand at the house door. 'As long as I may live to stand here,' cried she, 'who enters this door shall die!'

And the Justice called out, 'William of Cloudesley, yield yourself up!'

But William leaned from the window, bent his bow and shot. What happened? The arrow struck the Justice on the breast, but alas it broke in three. For the Justice was wearing a suit of mail under his coat.

'A curse on him who dressed you up in your coat today!' cried William. 'If your coat had been no better than mine, that arrow would have pierced you to the bone!'

And the Justice called out again, 'William of Cloudesley, put down your bow and yield yourself up!'

'A curse on him who counsels my husband so!' cried the doughty Alice, as she stood against the door with her pole axe.

'Set fire to the house!' shouted the sheriff. 'We'll burn the rascal and his wife and all his three children!'

Then men ran with burning brands. They set the house alight in many places, and the flames flew up both back and front, and on every side.

But William knotted sheets together, opened a back window, and quickly let down Alice and the three children.

'You have here all my treasure,' cried he, 'my wife and my three little ones. I pray you for the love of Christ do them no harm, but wreak all your wrath on me!'

32

And he drew his bow again, and leaning from the window shot arrow after arrow into the crowd below. Not one of those arrows missed its mark; with every arrow that he shot, a man fell. But the fire was all round him now, and soon he could shoot no more for his bowstring was burned in two.

Was William now to die a coward's death, there amid the flames? Not he! If he was to die, he would die fighting! And snatching up his sword and buckler, he ran out of the house, and charged the armed bands. Where the crowd was thickest, there ran William, hacking and hewing, smiting down one man, smiting down another man: the armed bands gave back before him; but they tore down doors and windows and hurled them upon him, felling him to the ground. And so they took him at last.

They bound him hand and foot and flung him into a deep dungeon. And the Justice cried out, 'Now Cloudesley, we have you and will hang you!'

And the sheriff said, 'I will make a new pair of gallows for you, my fine fellow. The gates of Carlisle shall be fast shut. No man shall come into the town until we have finished with you. You need hope for no help from Adam Bell and Clym of the Clough! Though they came with a thousand men, nay though they came with all the devils in hell, they should not enter!'

And away went the Justice and the sheriff, and left William lying bound in the dungeon.

Very early next morning the Justice rose up and hurried to the town gates. Yes, they were safely locked, and the porter was standing there with his keys. So, having warned the porter that he should open to no man until he got word, the Justice bustled off to the market place where workmen were busy setting up the new gallows. And having urged the workmen to make all haste, the Justice went home to his breakfast, chuckling as he went.

Amongst the crowd watching the putting up of the gallows was a little boy. Said he to one of the workmen, 'What are these new gallows for?'

And the workman answered, 'To hang a good yeoman, William of Cloudesley, more's the pity!'

Now this little boy worked for the town swineherd, and many

33

a time he had driven Alice's swine out to the woods to eat the acorns. And in the woods he had many a time met with William of Cloudesley, and always William was kind to him and saw to it that he didn't go hungry, but got a good dinner of venison. So the little boy crept away out of the market place and hurried to a far corner of the town, where he remembered to have seen a crack in the town wall. The crack wasn't wide enough for a man to get through, but it was just wide enough for the little boy's slim body. So he squeezed through that crack, and off with him fast as fast into the forest, and found Adam Bell and Clym of the Clough, and panted out the sad news that William was taken and condemned to death, and was to be hanged that very morning.

'Oh alas, alas!' cried Adam Bell. 'That ever we saw this day! Why must he have gone to Carlisle when we begged and begged him not to! We told him ill would come of it, and here's ill come indeed!'

But it was no good to stand there lamenting. They snatched up their bows and arrows, their swords and bucklers, and hurried off to Carlisle, to rescue their comrade if they might, or to die with him if they might not save him.

2

But when they came to Carlisle, of course they found the gates fast locked. What to do? They stood outside the gates and talked in whispers.

'We must try guile,' whispered Clym of the Clough. 'We must say we are messengers come from the king with a letter for the Justice. But will the porter believe us?'

And Adam Bell whispered, 'I have a letter in my pocket with a seal on it. We'll say it's the king's seal. I wager my life the porter is no clerk!'

Then Adam doubled up his fist and beat on the gate with all his might. The porter heard the noise and came running.

'Who's there?' cried he. 'And what do you want with your clamour enough to wake the dead?'

34

And Clym of the Clough answered, 'We are two messengers come from the king.'

'We have a letter to take to the Justice,' said Adam Bell. 'Let us in at once, that we may deliver our message, and return with an answer to the king.'

'I swear by heaven,' said the porter, 'that no man comes in until a false thief is hanged—him they call William of Cloudesley.'

'What, dolt!' cried Clym of the Clough. 'Are you mad? *I* swear by heaven that if we stand much longer here outside, it's *you* who will be hanged! Look, we have the king's seal! Will you flout that?'

The porter stooped and put his eye to the keyhole. Sure enough, there in Clym of the Clough's outstretched hand was a letter with a big seal on it. How could the porter tell one seal from another? He took off his hood and bent his knee.

'Right welcome is the king's seal,' said he, 'and welcome those who carry it!'

And he unlocked the gates.

Adam Bell and Clym of the Clough rushed in, seized upon the porter, struck him dead before he could so much as cry out, snatched the keys, locked the gates again, and hurried off to the market place.

The market place was thronged with jostling, gaping people, gathered from every quarter of the town to see William of Cloudesley hanged. In the middle of the square, rising gaunt and high above the heads of the crowd, stood the new gallows. Beside the gallows stood the Justice; and with him the sheriff and also the jurors whom they had persuaded to condemn William to death. And there in a cart, bound hand and foot, and with a rope round his neck, lay William.

The Justice called a young lad and bid him measure the length of William's body, and then go dig his grave, promising to give him in payment all William's clothes.

And the defiant William spoke up and said, 'It may be that he who digs my grave shall lie therein himself. I've known stranger things to happen!'

'For that saucy speech,' cried the Justice, 'I will hang you with my own hands!'

But in a corner of the market place, all unnoticed, Clym of the Clough and Adam Bell are standing with their bent bows in their hands. And even as the Justice speaks, two arrows fly. One arrow smites the Justice to the heart, the other pierces the sheriff through and through. Look! Both men fall dead, and the terrified crowd are running helter skelter. Clym and Adam run to William, cut the ropes that bind him: William leaps from the cart, seizes an axe from one of the town guard and lays about him. Now there is a running fight to reach the gates, William with his axe, Clym and Adam with their bows and arrows, amid a din of surging people, screams and shouts, and the sound of running feet.

But Clym and Adam have shot all their arrows; they cast their bows aside and draw their swords; and still retreating, but with their faces ever towards their attackers, they pass from street to street, approaching ever nearer the town gates. Added to the din now is the sound of horns and the clangour of bells rung backwards, for the Mayor of Carlisle has bid the horns to blow and the bells to ring to summon all true citizens to the fight. Here comes the mayor now, with a great troop of armed townsfolk. The mayor is brandishing a pole axe, he strikes William and breaks his buckler in two.

36

'Keep fast the gates, keep fast the gates!' shouts the mayor. 'These traitors shall not get out!'

But they are at the gates now, and Adam Bell has the keys. Swiftly he unlocks the gates, whilst William and Clym lay about them with their swords, holding back the press. The gates swing open, with one bound the three men are through, they are safe outside, they have locked the gates behind them. Let the mayor rave, let him order ladders to the walls, let the horns blow and the church bells ring backwards: the townsfolk have lost heart. They have no wish to go chasing to the forest after the three outlaws: they have enough to do now in seeing to the wounded, and burying their dead.

3

And deep in the forest, Adam Bell and Clym of the Clough and William of Cloudesley wash off the stains of battle and begin to think of dinner.

But what did they hear over there, a little way off among the trees? Surely it was a woman sobbing? And what was she saying amid her sobs?

'Oh my little children, my little children, what shall we do? Your father this day is hanged on high! We have searched and searched through the forest for his comrades, but we could not find them. Oh if I might but have had word with them, your father would not have died!'

Yes, it was Alice, William's wife, with her three little boys clinging to her skirts.

William ran and took Alice in his arms. 'Be comforted, dear Alice! You couldn't find my comrades, but my comrades found me. We might have died together like true brothers, but we have come safely off together, and all is well. So dry your eyes, and give thanks to these brave brothers of mine.'

'No need to speak further of that,' said Adam Bell. 'Here we are all starving, and our dinner yet running fast on its feet!'

So all three men took fresh bows and arrows, of which in the forest they had great store, and went to shoot the deer. Each of them shot a fat hart; they soon had the beasts skinned and cut up, a fire lighted and the meat roasting. And then, with wine in plenty, they all sat down to feast.

And when they had eaten their fill, William of Cloudesley said, 'Brothers, this life is all very well, but it can't go on for ever. My dear wife and my little children can't live here with us in the forest, I can't be seen in Carlisle, and if we are to be separated from one another, I would as soon be dead as not. I am going to our king, brothers, to sue for pardon. Alice and the two younger children shall stay in a nunnery meanwhile; but the eldest boy I will take with me. And he shall bring you word again of how I fare.'

'Nay, you shall not go alone,' said Adam Bell, 'for I will go with you.'

'And so will I,' said Clym of the Clough. 'What! after we have fought our battle side by side, do you think we shall desert you now? There may be danger; and in danger we three stand together.'

So the three of them set out for London, to petition the king. Alice and the two smallest boys went into a nunnery; but the eldest little boy, who, having reached the age of seven years, thought himself quite a man, would not be left behind, and he went with his father to London.

And when they reached London and came to the gates of the king's palace, they asked leave of no man, but marched right in. The porter ran after them shouting and scolding, demanding to know who they were; but they took no notice of him at all, and off with them across the courtyard and into the hall, where an usher came running to meet them.

'Yeomen, yeomen,' cried he, 'who are you, and what do you want? You will get us officers into sore trouble, behaving like this!'

'Sir, we are three outlaws of the forest, and we come to get us a free pardon from the king.'

So the usher brought them to the king. And they knelt down before him all three, and held up their hands.

They said, 'Sire, we beseech you to grant us mercy; for we have slain your fat fallow deer in many and many a place.'

38

The king said, 'What are your names?'

And they answered, 'Adam Bell, Clym of the Clough, and William of Cloudesley.'

'What!' cried the king. 'Are you those three rogues that men have told me of so often! Now, by heaven, you get no pardon from me! As I am king of this land, you shall all three be hanged!'

And he called his officers to secure them.

But as they were about to be led away, the queen came in. She looked on the three men and thought, 'How strong and vigorous they are, how frank and pleasant their sunburnt faces! Must such men as these be put to death?'

And she went to kneel before the king and said, 'My lord, when first you brought me into this land to be your wedded wife, you promised me that the first boon I should ask, you would certainly grant me. I have never asked you any boon till now; but now I do ask, and I pray you to grant it.'

The king took her by the hand and raised her up. 'Ask your boon, madam,' said he. 'It shall be granted.'

'Then good my lord, I pray you, grant me these three yeomen.'

'Madam,' said the king, 'you might have asked a boon of much more worth than these three rascals. You might have asked for towers and towns and unnumbered parks and forests.'

'But no boon so pleasant, and none so dear to me,' she said, 'as the lives of these three men.'

'By my faith,' said the king, 'I would rather have given you three good market towns! But since it is your desire, yes, I grant you their lives.'

Then the good queen rejoiced, and said, 'My lord, I thank you from my heart. And I do believe you will find them true men all three. But good my lord, speak some cheerful word to them that they may take comfort!'

The king didn't feel like speaking cheerful words, but he grunted out, 'Well fellows, I grant you grace. Wash yourselves. Go to dinner. And I will go to mine.'

So Adam Bell, Clym of the Clough and William of Cloudesley went off to the kitchen. And the king's servants set the tables in the great hall, and the king and his court sat down to dine. But they had scarcely begun to eat before messengers arrived from the north of England.

When the messengers were brought before the king, they knelt down and said, 'Lord, your officers bring you greetings from Carlisle.'

'And how fares my Justice of Carlisle?' said the king. 'And how fares my sheriff?'

'Sire, without a lie they are both slain, and many officers more.'

'And who has slain them?' cried the king.

'Sire, Adam Bell, Clym of the Clough, and William of Cloudesley.'

'The villains!' cried the king. 'The black-hearted villains! Alas, alas, had I but known this an hour ago, they had all been hanged! But now I have granted them grace, and bitterly I repent it!'

'Sire, we bring you a letter,' said the messengers.

The king took the letter. What did he read? The Justice slain, the sheriff slain, and the mayor of Carlisle Town; of all the constables of the town scarce one left alive; the beadles and the bailiffs, the sergeants, forty of the king's foresters—all dead! The outlaws had slain three hundred men and more!

'Take up the tables,' said the king. 'My heart is full of woe. I can eat nothing.'

'How is it possible,' said he to himself, 'that three men alone can have wrought all this havoc? I cannot believe it! I must see these fellows shoot!'

And he went out and summoned his best archers, together with Adam Bell and Clym of the Clough and William of Cloudesley to go to the shooting butts with him.

And they began to shoot. And though the king's archers sometimes missed their mark, the three outlaws never did.

'By heaven!' said William of Cloudesley, 'I reckon he's no good archer that shoots at *these* butts!'

'At what butts would you shoot then?' said the king.

'At such butts as men use in my part of the country,' said William.

40

'Let me see you shoot at such butts,' said the king.

So William and his two comrades went into a field and set up two hazel rods, four hundred yards apart. And William took his stand by one of the rods and pointed to the rod that stood four hundred yards away. 'I hold him to be an archer,' said he, 'who standing here can cleave yonder hazel rod in two.'

'There is none here can do that!' said the king. 'No man on earth can do it!'

'All the same I shall try, sire,' said William. And he set a long, tapered arrow to his bow:

Whang! There is the arrow now, flying across the field: and— yes—it has passed clean through the hazel wand and cleft it in two!

'You are the best archer that ever I saw!' cried the king.

'And yet, to gain your favour, I will endeavour a much harder task,' said William. 'I have a little son of seven years old, and heaven knows how dear he is to me! Now I will tie him to a stake and lay an apple on his head, take my stand six score paces from him, and with a broad arrow I will cleave that apple in two.'

'If you can do that,' said the king, 'I will reward you handsomely. But if you fail, you shall be hanged, queen or no queen! If you but touch his head or gown, I swear by all the saints in heaven, you shall be strung up—nay and not only you, but your two comrades also.'

'What I have said I will do, that I will do,' answered William.

And he got a stout stake and drove it into the ground. He took his little son, bound him to the stake, and turned the child's face from him, that he should not start. He set an apple on the child's head and stooped to whisper to him. 'Stand stiff and straight, my bonny boy, for as much depends on you as it does on me.' Then he bade the king's men to measure out a distance of a hundred and twenty yards from the stake. And there he took his stand.

'I pray you all, good people,' said he, 'to keep very still and very quiet. For he who shoots for a wager like this must have a steady hand.'

The watching crowd stood breathless, some of them wept,

41

some of them prayed. And though they marvelled at William's courage, they marvelled still more at the courage of William's small son, who stood at the stake motionless as a little statue, with back straight, arms stiff to his sides, and head proudly erect.

And William drew a fair broad arrow from his quiver, set the arrow to his bow, drew the bow, and shot.

Then indeed a roar went up from the crowd, a roar that was like the breaking of waves on a beach, roar upon roar, and again roar upon roar—for William had cleft the apple in two, and the little boy turned his head and laughed. William ran to release him from the stake, and caught him up in his arms.

'Oh my bonny boy, my bonny boy!' he cried, 'the victory is ours!'

'And may God forbid that you ever shoot at me!' said the king. 'From henceforth you shall carry *my* bow, and I make you chief ranger over all the north country. Your wages shall be eighteen pence a day.'

'And I will add another thirteen pence a day to that,' said the delighted queen, 'and your clothing to boot. Your two comrades shall be my yeomen of the guard, for never have I set eyes on comelier or braver men. Your little son shall be my cup bearer and serve me with wine; and when he comes to man's estate we will give him something better. And William,' said she, 'you must bring your wife to court, for I long to see her. She shall be chief gentlewoman to govern my nursery.'

But William said, 'My lord the king, and you my gracious lady queen, we three have the deaths of many men on our conscience. And though we acted in self-defence, our minds are not at rest. Give us leave, then, first to make a pilgrimage to Rome, there to seek absolution from his Holiness the Pope for all our sins. And when we are absolved, we will return to be your faithful servants.'

So William of Cloudesley, with his two comrades, Adam Bell and Clym of the Clough, set out on a pilgrimage to Rome. And there they relieved their troubled minds by confession to the Pope, and from him received absolution for all that they had done amiss. And so returned joyously to England. William fetched his wife and children and brought them to court. Alice made a splendid nurse, and her three little boys played happily with the queen's children.

And, true to their word, Adam Bell and Clym of the Clough and William of Cloudesley served the king faithfully and well for the rest of their lives.

43

CHILDE ROWLAND

THERE WAS A GOOD QUEEN who had three sons and one daughter. So one day the three princes went out to play ball in a field by the church; and their sister, Burd Ellen, went with them.

Well, the three lads were laughing and shouting and scrimmaging and scrummaging over the ball, till at last Childe Rowland, the youngest of the three, got that ball away from his brothers, and gave it such a tremendous kick that he sent it flying right over the top of the church tower.

'I'll fetch it back for you!' cried Burd Ellen. And she gave a jump over the churchyard wall, and away with her, fast as fast, round the church to find the ball.

Her three brothers waited. But Burd Ellen didn't come back with the ball. Maybe she couldn't find it? Maybe it was hidden in the long grass among the graves? So they all three jumped over the churchyard wall and ran about looking. But they didn't see that ball. Nor did they see Burd Ellen.

'Burd Ellen! Burd Ellen!' they called.

And there was no answer.

'Burd Ellen! Burd Ellen! Where are you?'

No answer.

Where *was* she? What could she be doing? Hiding from them? Ha! Ha! They would soon find her! They searched among the gravestones, they searched all round the church: they went into the church, they searched behind the pillars, behind the font, behind the screen, even under the altar. Not a sight of Burd Ellen.

'Burd Ellen, you saucy minx, we're going home!' they shouted.

And they went home.

'When she finds we're not to be troubled looking for her,' said they, 'she'll come back.'

But Burd Ellen didn't come back. Not that day, nor the next day. The three princes were very troubled, and the good queen, their mother, wept.

So the eldest prince said, 'I'll go to the Wizard Merlin. Maybe he can tell us where Burd Ellen is.'

And he went to the Wizard Merlin.

The Wizard Merlin opened his great book of magic: he turned the pages, he ran his finger down from sentence to sentence, and muttered to himself. The prince waited in silence.

And at last the Wizard Merlin looked up and spoke. 'The fair Burd Ellen has brought grief upon herself by going round the church widdershins, which is the opposite way to the sun. Because she did that, the Elfin King came and carried her away. She is now a prisoner in the Elfin King's Dark Tower. It would take a bold man to bring her back.'

'But I will bring her back,' said the eldest prince, 'or I will die in the venture. Only tell me what I must do.'

'There is one thing you must do, and one thing you must not do,' said the Wizard. And he told the prince what these things were.

And the prince set out for the Dark Tower.

The good queen, his mother, waited. The two princes, his brothers, waited. They waited long, long. But the eldest prince didn't come back.

So then the second prince said, '*I* will go to the Wizard Merlin, and ask what I must do to find Burd Ellen and my brother.'

And he went to the Wizard Merlin.

The Wizard Merlin opened his magic book, ran his finger down the pages, read, looked up and said, 'I told your eldest brother what he must do, and what he must not do; but he did not heed me. He is now a prisoner with Burd Ellen in the Elfin King's Dark Tower. It would take a bold man to bring those two back.'

'But I will bring them back,' said the second prince, 'or I will die venturing it! Only tell me what I must do.'

45

'There is one thing you must do, and one thing you must not do,' said Merlin. And he told the prince what those things were. And the prince set out for the Dark Tower.

The good queen waited. Childe Rowland waited. They waited long, long. But the prince did not come back.

So then Childe Rowland said, 'Mother, give me your blessing. I must set out to find Burd Ellen and my brothers.'

'Oh no my son, oh no my son!' cried the queen. 'Last year I had four children: now I have but one! If you are lost, then all is lost!'

But Childe Rowland begged and begged that she would let him go. He gave her no peace, night or day. And at last she sighed and said, 'Go then, and heaven be with you!' And she brought out his father's sword, that never struck in vain, and girding it round Childe Rowland's waist, she said the spell that gave that sword the victory.

And Childe Rowland went to the Wizard Merlin.

The Wizard Merlin opened his magic book, ran his finger down the pages, muttered, shook his head, and said:

'I told your brothers what they must do, and what they must not do; but they paid no heed. The Elfin King has them with Burd Ellen in his Dark Tower. It would take the boldest man in Christendom to win those three back.'

'But I will win them back,' said Childe Rowland, 'or I will die in the attempt. Only tell me how I must set about it.'

'My son,' said Merlin, 'there are but two things; one thing to do, and one thing not to do. And though those things sound simple, your brothers failed at them, and so may you. But get you gone, and go along and along and along till you come to the Land of Fairy. And once you have entered that land, the thing to do is this: whoever speaks to you, until you come to where Burd Ellen is, draw your father's sword that never struck in vain, and off with that one's head. That is the thing to *do*. And the thing *not* to do, is this: you will be hungry, you will be thirsty, but bite no bite, nor drink no drop in the Land of Fairy, or you will never win home again.'

Then Childe Rowland thanked the Wizard Merlin, and set out for the Dark Tower in the Land of Fairy. He went and he went and he went: he walked right out of this world into the

46

Land of Fairy, and there he met a horseherd with a multitude of horses. The horses' eyes shot out flames, and the horseherd's eyes were like coals of fire.

Said the horseherd, 'Whither away?'

Said Childe Rowland, 'To the Dark Tower, if you can tell me where it is?'

'Not I,' said the horseherd. 'I go no farther than my horses lead me. But walk on, walk on. You will come to a cowherd, and maybe he will know.'

Then Childe Rowland out with his good sword that never struck in vain: one stroke—off rolled the horseherd's head, and the horses galloped away.

Childe Rowland walked on. He went and he went and he went, till he came to a herd of grass-green cows, and a cowherd with them. The cows breathed out flames, and the cowherd's eyes glittered.

Said the cowherd, 'Whither away?'

'I seek the Dark Tower, if you can tell me where it is?'

'No,' said the cowherd. 'I can't. Go on farther and you will come to a henwife. She will tell you.'

Then Childe Rowland out with his good sword that never struck in vain: one stroke—the cowherd's head rolled from his body, and the herd of cows rushed off.

Childe Rowland walked on. He went and he went and he went, till he came to a poultry yard full of sky-blue hens. At the gate of the yard stood an old woman in a grey cloak.

Said the old woman, 'Whither away?'

Said Childe Rowland, 'To the Dark Tower, if you can tell me where I may find it?'

'That I can,' said the old woman. 'Go on but a little farther, and you will come to a round hill, all ringed about from bottom to top with green grass terraces. Walk round this hill three times widdershins, and each time say:

"Door, door, open thyself,
Let me come in!"

And on the third time of saying, a door will open in the hill,

47

and if you are nimble you may step inside. But if you delay, the door will shut again.'

Childe Rowland thanked the old woman. He was so happy to be near his journey's end that for a moment he forgot all about what he must do next. And even when he remembered, he hesitated. Was it a man's work to hack off the head of a harmless old woman? But then he thought on Burd Ellen and his two brothers, and hardened his heart. Out with the bright sword that never struck in vain: one blow, off went the old woman's head. It rolled into the poultry yard, the sky-blue hens flew up, cackling and screaming, and Childe Rowland took to his heels, and ran.

He ran, ran, ran, till he came to a round hill, ringed about from bottom to top with green grass terraces. He walked round the hill three times widdershins, saying each time:

'Door, door, open thyself,
Let me come in!'

And on the third time of saying, a door in the hill swung open: Childe Rowland darted in—well for him that he did not pause, for even as he got through it, the door banged on his heels.

Now he was standing at the end of a long passage, and it was neither dark nor light, but like an evening twilight. A warm wind blew along that passage, bringing with it the scent of apple blossom. Childe Rowland walked down the passage a long, long way, and came at last to two wide glittering doors. He pushed the doors open and went through, and they clanged shut behind him. Now he was in a great hall, with arching pillars of silver and a curved roof encrusted with jewels. The jewels shone and lit the hall with gold and ruby and diamond lights. And at one end of the hall, on an ivory couch, spread with cushions of rose-coloured velvet, sat Burd Ellen combing her yellow hair.

'Oh my brother, my brother!' cried Burd Ellen, 'why have you come here? This morning our mother had but one son, tonight she will have none. But sit you down, poor luckless fool, sit down by me whilst you may. For when the Elfin King comes back, your life is at an end.'

48

So Childe Rowland sat down by Burd Ellen on the ivory couch, and she told him how their two brothers had come before him to the Dark Tower, and how the Elfin King had cast his spells upon them and turned them into marble. 'And so he will do to you, brother,' said she. 'For once within this Dark Tower there's none gets out again.'

'Then I shall be the first that has come in and got out again,' said Childe Rowland boldly. 'And with me you shall go, and our two brothers also. But Burd Ellen, it is long, long, since I touched food, and I hunger and thirst. Give me to eat and drink, I pray you.'

Burd Ellen looked at Childe Rowland—oh so sadly! But she said no word, for she was under a spell and could not warn him. She got up, went through a little door behind the ivory couch, and soon came back again carrying a golden bowl full of bread and milk.

'Eat if you must, drink if you must, brother,' said she. And she put the bowl into his hands.

Childe Rowland lifted the bowl to his lips. He looked into Burd Ellen's eyes—why were those eyes so sad, so full of warning? Then he remembered what the Wizard Merlin had said, 'Bite no bite, nor drink no drop in the Land of Fairy, or you will never win home again.' And he dashed the bowl to the floor and cried out, 'Not a bite will I bite, not a sup will I swallow, till I set Burd Ellen free!'

And when he said that, the great glittering doors of the hall burst open, and in bounded the Elfin King. His white locks curled like snakes about his head, his green eyes flashed fire, and from top to toe he was clothed in silver armour. Waving his sword, screaming out threats and spells, he rushed upon Childe Rowland.

Childe Rowland sprang up from the ivory sofa. He drew his good sword that never struck in vain. 'Now by my mother's spell that gives this sword the victory, strike Bogle, if you dare!' he cried, and leaped to meet the Elfin King.

They fought, they fought, they fought. Up and down the hall they fought, and round and round: the silver pillars rang with the sound of the conflict, and the jewelled roof gave back the

49

echoes. But the magic in Childe Rowland's sword defied the Elfin King; and at last Childe Rowland had him beaten to his knees, and howling for mercy.

'Hand me your sword,' said Childe Rowland; 'release Burd Ellen from your spells, restore my two brothers to life, and let us all get quit of this Dark Tower and go on our way unharmed. Do this, and I will grant you mercy. Do it not, and with one stroke—off rolls your head.'

The Elfin King put his sword into Childe Rowland's hand. All the fierceness had gone from him: he was squealing like a frightened kitten. He went to a chest, lifted the lid, and took out a phial full of blood-red liquor. Behind the chest hung a curtain. The Elfin King drew the curtain aside, and there, each on a stone slab, lay Childe Rowland's two brothers, turned to marble. The Elfin King sprinkled the blood-red liquor from the phial onto their eyelids, and their eyes opened. He sprinkled the liquor onto their nostrils, and they drew breath. He sprinkled the liquor onto their lips, and they rose up and spoke.

'We have had a long sleep,' said they; 'and our dreams were strange ones.'

Then the Elfin King sprinkled some of the blood-red liquor onto Burd Ellen's breast, and released her from the spells that

50

bound her. 'And though I live ten thousand years,' he whimpered, 'I shall never get me as fair a maiden as you whom I have lost!'

Burd Ellen and Childe Rowland and their two brothers left him lamenting, and went from the hall and down the long passage, and out through the door in the round hill. The door clanged shut behind them; but before it shut, Childe Rowland flung the Elfin King's sword back into the passage.

And so they made their way speedily through the Land of Fairy, and back into their own world, and arrived home safely, to the great gladness of the good queen, their mother. Never again did any one of them set foot in the Land of Fairy; and never again did Burd Ellen go widdershins around a church.

THE CRAFTY FARMER

ONE MORNING a farmer got on his horse and set off to pay his rent. The way he had to go was lonely; and as he rode along he was keeping his eyes wide open, glancing from this side of the road to the other, lest a thief should be lurking among a clump of bushes, or behind a bit of a tumbledown wall. The farmer had tied his money in a bag, and strung the bag round his neck under his shirt; but still he didn't feel too safe, for a thief would as soon pull his clothes off him as not. And so that farmer was going warily, warily.

Well, when he came to the very loneliest part of the way, he heard galloping hoofs behind him, and a gallantly dressed gentleman caught up with him, and trotted along by his side.

'Well overtaken, my man!' said the gallant gentleman.

'Well overtaken, sir!' said the farmer. 'If so be that you are honest company. For I'm thinking this is an ill road to be travelling lonesome on.'

'An ill road it is!' said the gallant gentleman. 'And I for one am right glad to have company. Such tales as one hears of honest folk being robbed and left for dead in the ditch! How far might you be going?'

'Just some two miles more, good sir. I am a poor farmer, and I rent my ground. My half year's rent, sir, comes to forty pounds. But my landlord has been away travelling in foreign parts this year or more, and is but just come home. So that now I must pay him eighty pounds, and that large sum I am carrying to him.'

'Say you so?' exclaimed the gallant gentleman. 'But my good friend, you would have been wiser if you had kept that informa-

tion to yourself. There are many thieves about, you know; their
ears are sharp, they are cunning to hide—and what if one of
them should even now be near us, and have heard what you were
saying?'

What indeed! The farmer began to feel a little uneasy. Who
was this gentleman with his pistols at his belt, the feather
waving in his broad hat, and the devil-may-care look on his
face?

'Best way to have told nothing,' said the farmer to himself.
And then he had a crafty thought. And he laughed.

'Oh sir,' said he, '*I* have no fear of thieves! For I have sewn
that eighty pounds up safe in the lining of the saddle I sit on.
And who would think of searching for it there?'

'Truly man, you are wise!' said the gallant gentleman. 'As for
me, I travel light, and am worth no man's robbing. There is
nothing in my saddle bags but a change of linen. Nevertheless,
we best go warily here, for the road narrows and goes steeply
down hill; and, as you see, the hedges close in on either side. The
very place for thieves to lurk, if thieves there be.'

So they rode slowly on, down the steep hill, each man holding his horse on a tight rein. And in the very steepest part of that hill, when the farmer was watching his horse's steps and thinking no ill, what did that gallant gentleman do but spur on in front of him, wheel round, snatch a pistol from his belt, point it at the farmer's head, and cry out, 'Down off your horse, my man, for I must have that gold from out your saddle!'

The farmer slid from his horse. 'Oh sir, oh sir,' he cried, 'take pity on a helpless old man!'

'A helpless old fool, you should say!' answered the gallant gentleman. 'Here, hand me that saddle of yours, and hold my horse, whilst I cut your saddle open.'

The farmer was frightened, but he kept his wits about him. So, instead of handing the saddle to the thief, what did he do but toss that saddle over the hedge.

'Fetch it, if you must have it!' said he.

The thief scrambled over the hedge after the saddle, the farmer leaped onto the thief's horse, and off with him at full gallop. And as he rode away he heard the thief calling after him, 'Stop, stop, old man! Do but come back and I will give you half of all I have!'

'Come back, is it?' shouted the farmer. 'I may be a helpless old fool, but I'm not such an old fool as that! And I wish you joy of my eighty pounds!' cried he—and galloped right out of sight.

Meanwhile, behind the hedge, the thief had drawn his sword and was chopping the farmer's saddle to pieces. He chopped, and he chopped and he chopped, till the saddle was all in rags: but he didn't find that eighty pounds; no, he didn't find one halfpenny.

So the farmer got to his landlord's house, untied the bag from round his neck, and paid the landlord his eighty pounds. Then he set off home again, taking another way, that led him over fields and moors, and through bogs and prickly thickets: a long, long, roundabout way, but safer than the highroad where the thief might still be lurking.

The sun had set and night had come, and the farmer and the thief's horse that he rode were both well nigh spent by the time they arrived back at his little farm. His wife and his daughter had gone to bed, but they quickly rose and dressed, blew up the fire and got a meal ready. And the farmer, having stabled and fed the thief's horse, brought the thief's saddle bags into the kitchen.

'Wife,' said he, 'I have changed my mare for a better horse, and may be for something more.'

And he opened the saddle bags.

Oh ho! Ha, ha! What did he find inside those bags? Three hundred pounds in gold and three hundred pounds in silver! The farmer laughed and laughed; his wife and his daughter took hands and danced. They danced, and they danced, and they danced; and they sang, and they sang, and they sang.

Sang the wife, 'When you, my dearest daughter get wed, there's a dowry here for you!'

'A dowry here for me, a dowry here for me!' sang the daughter. 'When I and my dear young Sammy get wed, there's a handsome dowry for me!'

Farmer, wife, and daughter—they were three merry people who went to their beds that night.

TAM LIN

EVERYONE KNEW that the fairy man, Tam Lin, walked in the wood of Carterhaugh; and the earl who owned the wood had forbidden his daughter, Janet, and all the young maidens of his household, to go there.

But Janet was curious: she wanted to go to Carterhaugh wood and she didn't see why she shouldn't. She thought and thought about that wood, and the more she thought of it, the more she wanted to go there. And one autumn day, as she sat in her bower sewing a silken seam, the longing to go to the wood grew so strong that she threw down her needle and her silken seam, kilted her green skirt up above her knees, braided back her yellow hair, and off with her to Carterhaugh as fast as her running feet would take her.

It was a still, still sunny day in autumn; and here and there, under the green leaves of the wood, the wild roses were still in bloom. Very quiet it was, very mysterious to be there all alone, with not a bird stirring, and scarcely a leaf rustling.

Half afraid, half defiant, Janet sauntered on, wondering at the strangeness of the place, listening for any sound to break the stillness, shivering a little with the excitement of being where she was not supposed to be. . . . But, after all, this wood was as good as her own, for it was part of the property her father would leave her in his will: she had a right to be here in the wood, she could do what she liked with it; if she wished she could have it all cut down, she could break off the branches, she could pluck the flowers. . . .

And in a little spurt of defiance against the magic feeling of the place, she stooped to pick the flowers from a wild rose bush.

56

Oh heavens! She had scarcely plucked one rose from its stem when up out of nowhere, as it seemed, sprang a lad, the handsomest lad Janet had ever set eyes on—young Tam Lin himself!

And young Tam Lin was angry. 'Lady,' said he, 'leave that bush alone! How dare you pluck a rose, Janet, how dare you break the tree, how dare you come to Carterhaugh and ask no leave of me?'

And Janet, though she was sore afraid, answered proudly, 'I may come to Carterhaugh when I please, and I may pluck the roses and ask no leave of you or anyone. Carterhaugh is all my own. My daddy gave it to me.'

But young Tam Lin took her little white hand in his, and it seemed she must go where he wished, and do what he wished. He led her away, and away; he led her onto fairy ground, and there he told her that he loved her. And such was the magic and the charm about him, that before he let her go home again, Janet was as deep in love with Tam Lin, as any maiden could be.

And back in her father's hall, Janet, who had been the merriest of all the maidens, was now the saddest. She grew pale and sad with love longing. And 'oh' she said, and 'oh' she said, 'if my love were but an earthly knight, I wouldn't change him for any lord in the land! But alas, alas, my love is but a fairy elf, and oh what shall I do?'

What indeed? She felt she must see young Tam Lin at least just once more, or she would die of love longing. So again she kilted up her green skirt above her knees, braided back her yellow hair, and off with her to Carterhaugh wood as fast as her running feet would take her.

Dare she pluck another rose? No, she daren't. She stood all undecided in a great stillness, listening, wondering. Her hand touched the leaves of a low-growing branch, and in her nervousness she began to pluck at those leaves. But she hadn't plucked more than two, when up out of nowhere sprang young Tam Lin again.

'How dare you pull a leaf?' he said. 'How dare you break the tree? How dare you come to Carterhaugh again and ask no leave of me?'

57

'And if I come to Carterhaugh wood again,' said Janet, 'it is for love of you, Tam Lin. But tell me, oh tell me truly, for my heart is like to break, are you indeed an elfin born, or were you ever in holy chapel and baptised an earthly man?'

'Janet,' said young Tam Lin, 'listen to my story. A lord was my father, a lady my mother, even as it is with you. They had me christened in holy church, and trained me up in all knightly ways. But one day, as I was out hunting, there came a wind out of the north, a bitter, biting wind. So sharp was that wind, so deadly cold, that it froze my blood and robbed me of my senses. I fell from my horse. Then came the Queen of the Fairies, and carried me away to live with her in yonder green hill.

'The life in Fairyland is pleasant, Janet, the life in Fairyland is gay. None tires there, and none grows old. Indeed I would stay there forever, might I but stay in safety. But once in every seven years the fairies must pay a tithe of one of their knights to hell. And I am so comely and fair of face, Janet, I fear the next tithe will be myself. But you can save me, if you will.'

'I will save you, Tam Lin, yes, I will save you! Only tell me what I must do!'

Said Tam Lin, 'Tonight is Hallowe'en, Janet, tomorrow Hallow Day; and at the mirk of midnight the fairy host sets out to ride the whole country through. If you would win me free, you must take your stand at Miles Cross between the hours of twelve and one this night. Carry a flask of holy water with you, and sprinkle it in a circle. And in that circle you must take your stand till the fairy host sweeps by. For I shall be among that host, Janet.'

'But how shall I know you, Tam Lin, there in the darkness among a company of unknown knights?'

'To the first company of knights that rides by, Janet, say "no", and let them pass. To the second company that rides by, say "no" again, and let *them* pass. But when the third company passes by, there I shall be among them. Some knights will be riding on black horses, and some will ride on brown, but I shall ride on a milk-white steed with a gold star in my crown. They give me this honour because I was a Christian knight. My right hand will be gloved, my left hand will be bare, and at my side the Queen of Fairy herself will be riding, and her horse shines silver as the moon.

'Watch then, Janet: let the black horses pass, let the brown horses pass; but when the white horse passes, then quickly, quickly seize the bridle and pull the rider down. Fling your two arms round me, Janet, and as you love me, hold me well. They'll change me in your arms into this shape and that; but into whatever shape they change me, hold me fast, hold me fast! And when they turn me into a red hot bar of iron, cast me into the pool that stands by Miles Cross, and I shall be changed back into a naked man. Then quickly throw your green mantle over me, and I shall be won.'

'I will not fail you, Tam Lin,' said Janet.

And she went home to wait for night.

So, at the dead hour of night, there was Janet, standing at Miles Cross. She had sprinkled the holy water in a circle round her. Now she had only to wait. The stars shone above her, the pool lay at her side, and the reflections of the stars gleamed in its black depths. . . . Not a sound, but now and then the soft sigh of a night breeze.

And then, yes—far off—the jingle of bridles. And that sound made Janet as glad as ever she had been in her life.

The jingle of bridles grew louder and louder, but there was no other sound, for the host of fairy horses made no sound with their feet. Look! They are coming! A great company of shadowy riders sweeps past her. She makes no movement; she lets them pass on. Here comes a second company of shadowy riders: she makes no movement, she lets them go by. And here comes the third company. Watch now, Janet, watch for the white horse! This is the biggest company of all: some ride on black horses, and those she lets pass. Some ride on brown horses: those she lets pass. And then, ah, here comes the Fairy Queen herself, mounted on a moon-silver horse, and blazing with jewels. And at her side is a rider on a milk-white horse, and on his head is a crown of oak leaves in which gleams a golden star. His right hand is gloved, his left hand is bare: Janet leaps to seize the bridle of the milk-white horse: the white horse rears, whinnies, comes to a stand; Janet drags the rider from his seat, he slides

59

to the ground, Janet lets go the bridle, and clasps the rider in her arms.

Then rose an unearthly shriek from all the company. 'Tam Lin! Tam Lin! He's away! He's away!' The host of riders swarm about Janet, screaming out unutterable spells. It is no man now that Janet clasps in her arms, it is a flame of fire; but she holds that flame, fast, fast. The flame turns to a pillar of ice; she holds that pillar of ice fast, fast. The ice turns into a white swan that beats at her with its wings; she holds that swan fast, fast. The swan turns into a wolf that snaps at her with its jaws; she holds that wolf fast, fast. The wolf turns into a snake that writhes and hisses; she holds that snake fast, fast. The snake turns into a newt that tries to slip through her fingers; she holds that newt fast, fast. The newt turns into a deer that drives its antlers into her breast; she holds that deer fast, fast. The deer turns into a red hot bar of iron; she drops the bar of iron into the pool at her feet. The iron hisses and turns into a naked man: Janet stoops and wraps the man in her green mantle. Yes, she has won him at last: it is Tam Lin himself she clasps in her arms.

And oh but the Queen of Fairies is an angry woman!

'Janet has taken away the bonniest knight of all my company!' she cries. 'But if I had known but yesterday what I have learned today, Tam Lin, I would have taken out your heart of flesh and put in a heart of stone. And adieu, Tam Lin, adieu, Tam Lin! But if I had known a lady would win you away, I'd have taken out your bonny grey eyes and put in two eyes of wood! And had I the wit but yestere'en that I have bought this day, I'd have paid my tithe seven times to hell, before you were stolen from me!'

But stolen away from her young Tam Lin was, and the Fairy Queen could do nothing but ride off lamenting. She swept on with all her company, the white horse running riderless at her side. The last rider passed, the jingling of bridles grew fainter and fainter. It died away in the distance. Now there was no sound but the soft sigh of the night wind: the stars glittered in the sky, their reflections gleamed in the dark pool; and by the pool stood Janet and young Tam Lin, clasped in each others' arms.

60

So they went home together, and got married. And every one praised Janet for her brave deed, and rejoiced that young Tam Lin had been won back from the Land of Fairy.

KING ESTMERE

KING ESTMERE and Adler Young were brothers; and they were two of the boldest and bravest men that ever walked the earth.

So one day, as these two brothers sat drinking wine together in King Estmere's hall, Adler Young said, 'Brother, it is time you took a wife.'

'Brother,' answered King Estmere, 'there is no lady in my kingdom that I wish to marry.'

'That may well be,' said Adler Young, 'but your kingdom is not the world. There are many other kingdoms and many other kings. King Adland has a daughter whom all men praise for her goodness and beauty. If I were king here in your place, I would make that lady my queen.'

'Then give me your advice now, brother Adler. What messenger shall we send to speak of this matter with King Adland?'

'By my advice, no messenger at all,' said Adler Young. 'For messengers may be bunglers. You shall ride to King Adland's hall yourself, brother; and I will go with you.'

So off they set, the two of them, splendidly dressed in coats embroidered with gold and decked with jewels, off they set on two splendid horses to ride into the country of King Adland. And when they came to the gate of King Adland's castle, there was King Adland himself, leaning against the gate-post.

'God bless you, King Adland!'

'God bless you, King Estmere, and you, Adler Young! You are both dearly welcome to me!'

'You have a daughter,' said Adler Young; 'a daughter whom all men praise for her beauty and goodness. My brother would make her his wife, and queen of his kingdom.'

'Ah, King Estmere, but you are not the first to come on that errand,' said King Adland. 'Yesterday came the King of Spain wooing my lovely girl. And she said to him, "Nay, nay, nay!" And so I think she will say to you.'

'But the King of Spain is a wicked pagan!' said King Estmere. 'How could a lady but say nay to such a heathen hound? And if I am not to have your daughter for wife, I pray you that I may at least see her.'

So then King Adland led King Estmere and Adler Young into his great hall, and sent for his daughter.

There she is now, coming down the stairs into the hall—and oh, what a beauty! Her glittering golden hair hangs to her knees, and on every finger of her small hands she wears clear crystal rings. Fifty armed knights march before her, fifty ladies in silks and satins walk behind her, and fifty pages in flowered tabards bring up the rear. It is indeed a proud procession! But the lady herself is by no means proud. She trips up to King Estmere and greets him with a lovely smile.

'You are welcome, King Estmere,' says she. 'You are indeed right welcome to me! And if you love me as you say, the matter you have come about shall very soon be settled.'

King Estmere falls on his knees. He kisses her little hand. He is enraptured.

But King Adland frowns and shakes his head. 'My dear daughter,' says he, 'I beg you to pause and consider well what you are about. What was it the King of Spain said yesterday? Didn't he threaten to pull down my castle walls and carry you off by force if you would not consent to be his wife? . . . I don't know that I can blame him, either! Nor perhaps can you, if you will but look at yourself in the glass.'

But the lovely lady laughed and said, 'Your castles and your towers stand firm and strong, Father; we need not fear the King of Spain. But now plight me your troth, King Estmere. Swear by heaven and your right hand that you will take me as your wife, and make me queen of your land.'

And King Estmere held up his right hand, and swore by heaven that he would do just as she wished.

Who now so glad of heart as King Estmere? He bids farewell

63

to his lovely lady, and sets off with Adler Young to his own country. He is off to fetch a great train of dukes and lords and knights to attend the wedding ceremony.

But King Estmere and Adler Young had ridden scarce more than a mile on their homeward journey, when the King of Spain arrived back at King Adland's castle, bringing an army with him. Today he would marry King Adland's daughter, tomorrow he would carry her home, or his army should raze King Adland's castle to the ground.

The princess looked out of her window: there was the Spanish army encamped all round the castle. She tiptoed to the head of the stairs and looked down into the great hall: there was the ruffianly King of Spain surrounded by his armed knights. What could she do? She called a little faithful page to her.

'Go out into the courtyard, my little lad,' said she. 'Go through the castle gates. Go to and fro among the Spanish troops, and look about you wonderingly. No one will question a little lad come to admire the Spanish troops. But edge you through them cunningly; and when you are past them all, take to your heels and run. Soon you will come to King Estmere, riding along the way. Tell him from me that he must either turn again and fight, or go home and lose his lady.'

The little page was swift to do his mistress's bidding. He stole out of the castle gates; he loitered here and there among the Spanish troops; he gaped at their bright swords, their plumed helmets, their steel-ringed coats of mail. The soldiers laughed to see the little lad, wide-eyed with admiration, as quietly, quietly he slipped from rank to rank, until he was beyond them all. Then he took to his heels and ran, no greyhound faster, till on the road in front of him he saw King Estmere and Adler Young trotting gaily on their splendid horses. And then he shouted loud:

'Tidings, tidings, King Estmere!'

King Estmere reined up his horse.

'What tidings now, my little lad?'

'You had not ridden scarce a mile, scarce a mile from the castle, when in came the King of Spain. Yes, in he came with his bold barons, and his knights, and an army of fighting men.

64

And so my lady greets you well, and bids me say that you must either turn again and fight, or go home and lose your lady.'

King Estmere turned to Adler Young: 'What do you advise, brother? Shall we turn and fight, we two against an army? Or must we now go home, and I lose my lovely queen?'

'Nay, we will not go home by my counsel,' said Adler Young. 'I have thought of a way to free your lady. You remember how when I was a boy our mother sent me to school? That school, brother, was a school of wizardry. And I learned magic there, and the use of many a herb. And in that field yonder I see a herb that will serve us now. We have but to eat its leaves and it will change the colour of our faces from white and red to darkest brown. Moreover, so strong is its magic that when we have eaten those leaves, there is not a sword in all the world will dare to wound us. . . . Now you, my little lad,' said he to the page, 'away with you back to your mistress and tell her we will not fail her. And you, brother, stay here on the road, and I will go to the field and pluck the herb.'

So the page turned and ran back to King Adland's castle: King Estmere waited on the road with the horses, and Adler Young went into the field. When he came back, he was bringing, besides the herb, a harp, two flat caps and two sombre-coloured robes.

'And where and how I got these things, you mustn't ask, brother,' said he, 'for it was all done by magic. Now you shall be a harper, brother, come from the north country. And I will be your boy, and carry your harp. You shall be the best harper that ever touched a harp, and I shall be the best singer that ever sang in any land. And when we have eaten of the herb, brother, there will be a sign written on our foreheads that will say to all who would attack us, "Beware! Beware!"'

'Come, now we will eat.'

Then Adler Young took the herb and broke it into two equal pieces. One piece he ate himself; one piece King Estmere ate. And immediately the complexion of their faces changed from red and white to darkest brown, as if they had been wandering in foreign lands and scorched with the sun.

'Brother,' said Adler Young, 'do you see a sign written on my forehead?'

65

'Yes,' answered King Estmere. 'I see a sign that says "Beware"! I see it, but not with my eyes—and yet I see it.'

'And on your forehead I see a like sign,' said Adler Young. 'Now we will go back to King Adland's castle and win your bride.'

Then they put on the sombre-coloured robes over their gay coats, covered their bright hair with the flat caps, leaped onto their horses and galloped back to King Adland's castle.

As wandering minstrels they passed through the throng of the King of Spain's army without questioning, and came to the gates of the castle. And there was the porter, leaning against the gate-post, watching the soldiers.

'God bless you, good porter!' said King Estmere.

'God bless you, my masters!' said the porter. But he was staring at them in a puzzled kind of way, so King Estmere said, 'We are harpers out of the north country, come to play at a merry wedding feast. So let us pass, good man!'

'Harpers you seem to be,' said the porter doubtfully. 'But if your colour were white and red instead of darkest brown, I would say that King Estmere and his brother had come back to the castle.'

Then King Estmere took a gold ring from his purse and laid it on the porter's arm.

'All we ask of you, brave porter, is to let us pass, and speak no ill of us.'

The porter looked doubtfully and long at the ring. He looked hard and long at King Estmere. Then he slowly opened the gates and King Estmere and Adler Young rode through. They rode across the court, they rode through the castle door, they rode right into the great hall where a crowd of people was gathered. The princess was there, seated at the high table beside King Adland; the King of Spain was there, seated beside the princess. The princess's ladies in waiting were there, and her knights and her squires, and her pages. And all round the walls, and leaning against the pillars, stood the armed knights and barons of the King of Spain's bodyguard.

King Estmere gave them not a glance, he rode his horse straight up to the high table, and there he leaped from the

66

saddle. The horse, covered with foam from its hard gallop, shook its head, and the froth from its bit flew onto the King of Spain's beard.

The King of Spain started to his feet. 'Is it fit that a harper should stable his horse in the king's hall?' he cried. 'Away with you, proud harper, away with you to the stables, and put your horse in a stall!'

But King Estmere only laughed. 'My lad is naughty,' said he. 'He has no manners, and never does the proper thing. Is there any man in this hall who is able to beat my lad for me?'

'You speak proud words,' said the King of Spain. 'There's many a man in this hall will beat your lad, and beat *you*, into the bargain!'

'Then let that man come forward,' said King Estmere. 'And when he has well beaten my lad—why then he shall beat me!'

So then one of the King of Spain's bodyguard stepped forward. In his coat of mail and his glittering helmet, and with his drawn sword in his hand, he marched up to Adler Young. But when he looked into Adler Young's face, he gave a cry, dropped his sword and slunk away.

'How now, man!' cried the King of Spain. 'What ails you? Strike man, strike!'

'My gracious king,' stammered the soldier, 'there is a sign written on the man's forehead, and the sign is magic! For all the gold under heaven I dare not venture near him!'

Then King Estmere took his harp and began to play a sweet music. And when the princess heard that music, she got up to leave her seat, but the King of Spain caught her by the sleeve and made her sit down again.

'Stop that playing, you proud harper!' he shouted. 'For if you go on playing as you have begun, it seems you'll win my bride from me!'

But King Estmere struck the harp again, and played sweet music. And the princess laughed and laughed.

'Sell me your harp, proud harper,' said the King of Spain, 'and you shall have as many gold guineas as there are knights in the hall.'

'And what will you do with my harp, King of Spain, if I should sell it to you?'

'I will have one of my own musicians to play it to my wife and me after we are married,' said the King of Spain.

And King Estmere answered, 'Sell me your fair bride, King of Spain, and I will give you as many gold guineas as there are leaves on a tree.'

'And what would you do with my fair bride if I should sell her to you?' laughed the King of Spain.

And King Estmere answered, 'What would I do with your fair bride but take her home with me. For it is more seemly for a lady fair to wed with me than you.'

Then he struck the harp again, and played a soft, sweet music. And Adler Young began to sing:

'O lady, lady, bend your ear
And listen whilst I sing!
O lady this is thy own true love,
No harper but a king.
O lady this is thy own true love,
As plainly thou mayst see,
And I'll rid thee of that foul paynim
Who parts thy love and thee.'

And with that, Adler Young drew his sword, leaped upon the King of Spain, and smote off his head.

Immediately the hall was in an uproar.

'Traitors! Traitors! They have killed our king!'

With drawn swords, from every side, the King of Spain's fighting men rushed upon King Estmere and Adler Young. But when they came near they all fled back with shrieks of terror. They could not face the magic sign written on the two men's foreheads. They fled from the hall, with King Estmere and Adler Young at their heels; they fled through the castle court, and out through the castle gates; they rushed among the soldiers encamped outside:

'To horse, to horse!' they shouted. 'Save yourselves! All hell is risen against us!'

The soldiers needed no second bidding: one glance at King

68

Estmere and Adler Young was enough. Some on horseback, some on foot, they all fled fast away. The sound of galloping hoofs and running feet dwindled into distance; and soon all was quiet.

Then King Estmere and Adler Young went back into the castle. And at some magic words spoken by Adler Young their faces turned again from darkest brown to red and white. They threw off their sober minstrels' garments; and when they came into the hall they were all in glittering gold.

'Lady,' said King Estmere to the princess, 'I thought to bring my dukes and lords and knights to grace our wedding feast. But fate has willed it otherwise.'

And the princess answered, 'What do we need with your dukes and your lords and your knights? The bridegroom is here, the bride is here, the bride's father is here to give us his blessing, the priest is here to marry us, and some ring I am sure you have to put upon my hand.'

So they two were married, and they feasted and made merry. And King Adland blessed them, and gave them a splendid coach to carry them back to King Estmere's kingdom, and a retinue of knights and squires to ride before and behind them. And so they got safely home and were received by King Estmere's people with great rejoicing. Long they lived and happily, with Adler Young always at their side to advise and protect them with his magic.

ALISON GROSS

SEE THAT TOWER up yonder? That's where Alison Gross lives; and she's the ugliest witch ever you set eyes on, or ever will. So one day this old hag came up with me as I was out walking. And she was all one grin.

'Good day to you, my pretty lad,' says she. 'You come up to my tower, and I'll show you all my treasures.'

Well I knew she had treasures, piles of them; and I was curious. So I promised to come up that evening. And as I was setting out, my sister Maisrie said, 'Where are you going?'

'Up to call on Alison Gross and see her treasures,' says I.

'Don't go!' says Maisrie.

'Why not?' says I.

'Because sure as I'm alive she'll put a spell on you,' says Maisrie.

'Pooh!' says I. 'What harm can the old hag do me if I keep my wits about me?'

And I went.

Everything was marvellous inside that tower: there were gold chests and silver chests, the walls were hung with coloured velvets, and the ceiling sparkled with jewels. And the old thing took me by the hand and said, 'You're welcome lad, welcome as flowers in May, for sure there's no bonnier lad in all the world, and it does my old eyes good just to look on you, so it does. Only your hair wants combing, for the wind has ruffled it.'

'Well then, comb it,' says I, all cock-a-hoop and cheeky.

So she fetched a golden comb and passed it through my hair; and after that I can't say what happened. I found myself sitting on her knee, and she stroking my head, and myself all in a maze.

70

And the next thing she was saying was that I should be her
sweetheart, and promising me everything fine under the sun.
She set me down in a chair, went rummaging through a chest,
and brought out a mantle of scarlet cloth, fringed with gold and
silver, and all embroidered with golden flowers. She draped the

mantle over my shoulders and said, 'A goodly gift for a goodly laddie; and it's yours if you'll be my lover.'

Her grinning face was so close to mine that I could feel her breath all hot on my cheek. It gave me a turn! I shook the mantle off my shoulders, and cried out, 'Get away, you ugly witch! Let me be! I won't be your lover, and I wish I'd never come here, so I do!'

I wanted to get up and run out then, but seems I couldn't. Where I sat, there I had to stay: my legs had gone weak.

So next she showed me a silk shirt with pearls all round the neck band. And she held it up to me and said, 'If you'll be my lover, this shirt is yours.'

But I cried out, 'Hold off, you ugly witch!'

And I pushed the shirt from me.

Well, she only grinned, rummaged in the chest again, and brought out a gold cup encrusted with glowing jewels.

'See here,' says she, holding the cup before my dazed eyes, 'isn't this a gift worth having? Come on now, laddie, one kiss and the cup is yours!'

What could I do? I struck the cup out of her hand and shouted 'Keep off! Let me be, you ugly old witch! I wouldn't once kiss your ugly mouth, no, not for gold or jewels or any treasure the world holds!'

My word! When I said that, her grins turned to scowls. She spun round like a top; she snatched up a grass-green horn from the chest and blew three loud blasts. 'I swear by the moon and all the stars that shine,' she yelled, 'that I'll make you rue the day you were born!'

And then she picked up a silver wand and spun round and round three times, hitting me with the wand and screeching out words that made my blood run cold. My brain whirled, my head swam, and I fell down senseless. . . .

And when I came to myself—where was I, and *what* was I? I was changed into an ugly little dragon, and I was toddling round and round a tree.

For a whole week I did nothing but toddle round and round that tree. And then, on Saturday night, who should come to me but my sister Maisrie, carrying a silver basin and a silver comb.

72

She sat down, took my poor ugly head on her knee, and washed it with water from the silver basin. Then she took the silver comb, and combed down the horrid tufts of hair that stuck up like little prickly bushes all over my head. But that was all she could do. She couldn't give me back my proper shape; and though my heart was heavy as a lump of lead, I knew that I'd sooner be a dragon toddling round that tree forever and a day, than have once kissed Alison Gross.

So it went on, week after week; and every Saturday night my sister Maisrie came with her silver basin and her silver comb to wash and comb my head. And no one else came near me. . . .

Until the last day of October, which was Hallowe'en, and moonlight. On that night I pricked up my ears, for I heard, at first far off, but coming every moment nearer, the soft thud, thud of hoofs, the jingling of harness, and the tinkling of little bells. And then I saw a glorious company of riders on white horses sweeping along in the moonlight past my tree.

It was the fairy court riding by; and in the midst of them rode the Fairy Queen, shining and shimmering like moonlit water. When she saw me, she reined up her horse, and stepped down onto a grassy bank that was covered with daisies. Not a word did she say, but she came to me, lifted me up in her milk white hands, sat her down among the daisies, and stroked me three times over her knee.

Just three strokes she gave me: and then she was gone, and all her fairy host was gone with her.

But I wasn't an ugly little dragon any more, and I wasn't toddling about the tree. I was standing on the daisied bank in my own proper shape.

So I went home rejoicing. And from that day to this I've never come face to face with Alison Gross. If I but catch a glimpse of her—a mere speck in the distance—why then I take to my heels.

YOUNG BEKIE

THERE WAS A GALLANT ENGLISH KNIGHT—Young Bekie
was his name—and he crossed the sea to serve the king of
France.

Well, well, he hadn't been at the French court a twelve month
before he fell in love with Burd Isbel, the French king's only
daughter. And he made no secret of his love, either! The
impudence of it! The French king flew into a rage, and flung
Young Bekie into a deep dark dungeon.

Poor Young Bekie—they fed him on bread and water, they
gave him no light, no bed; he lay down at night to sleep on the
cold, cold stones, and the mice and the rats scampered over
him, and nibbled off mouthfuls of his yellow hair to line their
nests.

Burd Isbel had not said 'aye' to Young Bekie's love; but then
neither had she said 'nay'. And now that he had been flung into
prison for her sake, her heart went out to him. When she went
out to take the air, she would often find herself taking the way
that led past the prison house, and lingering outside its sullen
walls, and pitying, and wondering.

And then one day—oh dear!—she heard moans within the
prison; and having glanced quickly round to make sure no one
was watching, she put her ear to the dark, dark wall of the
prison, and listened.

This is what she heard:

'Is there no one in the wide world to pity me and set me free?
If an earl would unlock my prison door, I would be his servant
for ever more, to run at his stirrup-foot. Or if a dame would
unlock my prison door, I would swear to be her son. And if a

74

maiden would unlock my prison door, I would wed her with a ring. I would give her halls, I would give her bowers. I would clothe her in silks and satins and share with her all I have.'

That night Burd Isbel couldn't sleep for thinking of Young Bekie. So she rose from her bed and went softly downstairs, tiptoeing on bare feet. And that was not for lack of shoes and stockings, nor for lack of time to put them on; but it was for fear lest the king her father should wake and demand of her where she was going. She took the keys of the prison house from the nail where they hung, she took a candle and a tinder box, she went out of the palace, and stole across the court to the prison door, she unlocked that door and went in.

Then she lit her candle.

The mice and rats scuttled away under her feet: Young Bekie started up—lean, ragged, covered with dirt, with wild eyes, unshaven beard, and hair half chewed away. Young Bekie! Could it be Young Bekie? The handsome, elegant, merry knight who had sworn before them all how dearly he loved her? Burd Isbel's heart melted with pity. And now she knew she loved Young Bekie truly.

Quickly she brought him water to wash, and a razor to shave with. She took scissors from her belt and a comb from her pocket, and gently, lovingly, trimmed and combed his shaggy hair. Then she hurried away and came back with food and wine and five hundred pounds in gold.

'My own horse is standing at the gate,' she whispered, 'and with him wait my leash of hounds. Take the gold, take the horse, take the hounds, and get you gone! Only I pray you look well after the biggest hound, whose name is Hector, for he is very dear to me.'

'No, no, no!' cried Young Bekie. 'How can I go and leave you here, when I love you more than life?'

But Burd Isbel told him that if he stayed now, they both were like to lose their lives, for the king her father would never forgive her for what she had done. Somehow, somewhere, they would meet again. And they broke a gold ring between them and took a solemn oath that before three years had come and gone, they would find each other and get married.

75

So, with many a kiss, and many a promise that they would remain true to each other, they parted. Young Bekie leaped on horseback and galloped to the sea coast, followed by the leash of hounds. And Burd Isbel tiptoed back to bed.

What clamour, what uproar next morning when it was found that Young Bekie had broken prison and got away! And no one more surprised, and no one more callous-seeming, than the artful Burd Isbel. Oh yes, if caught he would be hanged, no doubt, and maybe serve him right. For though he was a pretty young fellow, he was somewhat too big for his boots. . . .

'Hanged! Of course he will be hanged!' cried the king. And he sent out armed riders with orders to scour the country, and bring back the prisoner, alive or dead.

But they didn't find Young Bekie. He had reached the coast; and there, with some of the gold Burd Isbel had given him, he had hired a ship, and now with his horse and his leash of hounds he was sailing fast home to England.

And he reached home in safety; and when he got back to his father's hall, there were great rejoicings.

'Now my son,' said his father, 'you shall take a wife, and wander into foreign parts no more. For you are my only son; all this great estate will one day be yours, and I would see you blessed with a wife and children before I die.'

Young Bekie was quite willing to stay at home for the present, and learn to manage the estate. But he thought of Burd Isbel and his solemn oath to her, and he said he had no mind to take a wife.

'We will get you to change your mind in a few months,' said his father.

But Young Bekie didn't change his mind, either in a few months, or in many months. And when his father began to fret and fume, and speak of a young duchess who was the very wife for him—why then Young Bekie told of his love for Burd Isbel, and of his sufferings in prison for her sake, and of how she had set him free.

'She is my love, and she must be my wife, for I will have no other,' said he.

What! Wed the daughter of a dastardly Frenchman who had

clapped him into prison and well nigh starved him to death! Young Bekie's father was horrified. No, no, Young Bekie must put such an idea out of his head, and marry the young duchess. Why, the marriage was as good as arranged, his father said.

But Young Bekie said no, and no, and no. And the disagreement between him and his father became more hot and bitter with every day that passed. Until the father said that if Young Bekie wouldn't do what he was told, why then he washed his hands of him. Yes, he would turn him out of doors, and leave all the estate to his cousin John.

'And you can go and marry your French princess, and the two of you can beg your bread from door to door!' he cried.

Young Bekie went out into the garden to think things over. And he was very sorrowful.

'Oh me, alas!' said he to himself, 'what can I do? I would willingly be a beggar for Burd Isbel's sake! But what would that profit me? A beggar cannot marry a king's daughter. As a beggar I would be ashamed even to approach her. No, I cannot go to Burd Isbel, nor can she come to me.'

And he decided that he must do as his father wished, marry the young duchess—and be miserable for the rest of his life.

So the wedding day was fixed. . . .

And one night, as Burd Isbel lay peacefully sleeping, and dreaming of Young Bekie, something leaped onto her bed with such a bounce that it woke her up. And there she saw a tiny little man, dressed in green, dancing up and down on the counterpane. She could see him quite plainly although it was dark, for he was lit up from inside.

'Who are you?' cried Burd Isbel. 'Where have you come from? What are you doing here?'

'Who am I indeed?' shrilled the tiny little man. 'I'm the Billy Blind, I am, as you ought to know full well! Where have I come from? I've come from behind your hearth, where I live. What am I doing here? I'm waking you up, that's what I'm doing. How can you lie there, how can you sleep so sound, when tomorrow is Young Bekie's wedding day?'

Burd Isbel jumped out of bed then. She wrung her hands and cried, 'Oh what shall I do? What *shall* I do?'

77

'Stop wringing of your hands, for a start,' said the Billy Blind. 'And listen to me, to go on with. We must stop this wedding, mustn't we? Well then, haste and dress yourself! Put on your best robes of scarlet velvet, rouse two of your maids and dress them in dainty green. Set rings on all your fingers, and gold and jewels in your hair; and do the same by your two maids. And let all of you wear girdles crusted thick with such gems as would buy an earldom. Then away to the river bank with the three of you, and there you'll see a little ship come sailing to the land. You'll set your foot in that little ship and cry, "Hail ye, Domine!" And I myself will be in the ship to sail you to the river mouth and across the sea.'

Burd Isbel hurried to do what the Billy Blind told her. She dressed herself in her scarlet robes and her two maids in dainty green; and the three of them put on coronets that sparkled with gold and jewels, and girdles encrusted with more glittering gems than would buy an earldom. And so, in all their rich array, they stole out of the palace and away to the river bank.

It was dark, dark night, with neither moon nor stars to guide them; but they could hear the river gurgling by. And as they stood and waited and listened to the sound of the water, they saw far off, but coming swiftly nearer, the glimmer of a silver sail. Yes, there was a little boat rushing towards them. And it came to the bank where they stood.

'Hail ye, Domine!' cried Burd Isbel, and leaped into the boat; and after her hurried the two maids. And there was the Billy Blind curled up in the stern, with the rudder in his tiny hand. And the boat might have been a living thing, the way it swung back from the shore, and sped down the river, away and away to the river mouth, and away and away across the sea.

Before morning the little boat had reached the shores of England. Before noon Burd Isbel and her two maids stood at the gates of the lordly castle that was Young Bekie's home. The gates were wide open, the court was thronged with horses and carriages and servants in splendid liveries; and from within the castle came the sound of music and singing. From all that she saw and heard Burd Isbel understood well enough that this was Young Bekie's wedding day.

And she took three guineas from her pocket and gave them to
the porter, who stood by the open gates, gaping at her and her
two maidens in astonished admiration. 'For surely,' thought he,
'they be three queens, and where can they have come from?'

'Porter,' said Burd Isbel, 'where is the bridegroom?'

'Upstairs with the bride, my lady,' said the porter. 'Where
else should he be, and this his wedding day?'

Then Burd Isbel put into the porter's hand her half of the
golden ring that she and Young Bekie and broken between
them.

'Go, carry this to the bridegroom,' said she, 'and tell him there is a lady at his gate would fain speak with him.'

The porter took the gold half ring and hurried into the castle, and up the stairs, and into the hall among the wedding guests. And there he knelt down at Young Bekie's feet.

'Get up, get up, proud porter!' said Young Bekie. 'Why do you kneel to me?'

And the porter said, 'Sir, I have been porter at your father's gate these thirty years and more. But there's three ladies stand there now, the like I never saw. One of them is dressed in scarlet robes, and two in dainty green; the jewels that sparkle in their hair would put the sun to shame, and their girdles are set more thick with gems than would buy an earldom.'

'Well, well,' laughed the bride, who was dressed all in gold. 'If there are fair ladies at the gate I'll warrant there are fairer ladies in this hall!'

And the bride's mother spoke up angrily. 'If you had learned good manners, you proud porter,' said she, 'as I see you have not, you would at least have excepted our lovely bride!'

'My lady,' said the porter, 'the lovely bride is fair enough, and I wish her all that's good. But the lady standing at the gate outshines all ladies upon earth. And she bid me give you this, my lord,' said he to Young Bekie; 'and would fain speak a word with you.'

And he put the gold half ring into Young Bekie's hand.

And when Young Bekie saw that half ring, he gave a shout of joy and rushed from the hall. Down the stairs he bounded, five stairs at one leap, and out to the gates, and flung his arms about Burd Isbel and kissed her again and again.

'Oh Young Bekie,' said she, 'have you forgotten the vow you made to me when I took you out of prison? When I gave you my own good horse and my leash of hounds? When I gave you all I had, even my favourite hound, Hector? . . . But it seems a dog is more faithful than a man,' said she. For there was Hector, who had followed Young Bekie down the stairs, and was now leaping around Burd Isbel, and crouching at her feet, and leaping up again, barking and whining with joy.

Young Bekie had no word to answer: he could only sob. He

took Burd Isbel by the hand and led her up into the hall, followed by her two maidens. And all the wedding guests fell silent with astonishment.

And Young Bekie turned to the bride's mother and said, 'Take home your daughter, good dame, and my blessing go with her! For I must marry my Burd Isbel, who has loved me long and has crossed the sea for my sake.'

And again the bride's mother spoke up angrily. 'Is it the fashion in your country, Young Bekie, to fetch a bride on a May morning and send her back home at noon?'

'No, it is not the fashion in any country,' said Young Bekie. 'But a man must marry the one he loves. And see—there is my cousin John, a handsomer man than I!'

Then Young Bekie went to kneel down at the young duchess's feet. 'Lady,' said he, 'if you will wed my cousin John, there's a wedding present of five hundred pounds waiting for you.'

But the young duchess laughed and said, 'You may keep your money, Young Bekie. I want no gift from you. Your cousin John was my first love. And I think my mother had as much trouble to persuade me to this wedding as your father had with you!'

And all this time Young Bekie's father was gazing and gazing at Burd Isbel. Yes, he had to admit that Young Bekie was right; for never in his life had he set eyes on a maiden more to his liking than the lovely Isbel.

So, instead of one unhappy wedding that day, there were two merry ones. And who should come and dance at the wedding but the Billy Blind? The Billy Blind made them all laugh with his antics; and he told Burd Isbel that he was never going back to France. For he was her own Billy Blind: and where her hearth was, there he would make his home.

THOMAS THE RHYMER

ONE HOT SUMMER DAY, Thomas the Rhymer was lying, with his harp beside him, on Huntley Bank, thinking lazy thoughts, and now and then making up a rhyme or two. It was very peaceful where he lay: bees hummed, leaves rustled, the river slipped drowsily by. Thomas was almost asleep, when he heard a sound that made him open his eyes. It was the pretty tinkling of hundreds of little bells.

Thomas sprang to his feet. He was wide awake now. A horse and a rider were coming towards him: the horse was white as milk, and from every lock of its mane hung nine and fifty little silver bells. The lady who rode the horse was wearing a skirt of grass green silk and a velvet mantle, and her hair sparkled with jewels: but her face—never had Thomas seen a face so fair, so strange, so unearthly in its beauty. Surely such beauty must be of heaven, not earth!

The lady galloped straight up to him, and reined in her milk-white steed.

And Thomas pulled off his cap, went down on one knee, and cried out, 'All hail, most gracious lady, Queen of Heaven!'

But the lady laughed. 'Oh no, oh no, Thomas,' said she. '*I* am no Queen of Heaven! I am but the Queen of fair Elfland, come to pay you a visit. For I would have you play your harp and sing your songs to me in Elfland.'

And when she had said that, she was out of the saddle in a twinkling, and standing by Thomas, smiling and looking deep into his eyes.

'Thomas,' says she, 'would you dare to kiss my lips?'

Well, well, if she wasn't the Queen of Heaven, Thomas felt no awe of her. And then and there he kissed her on the lips.

And the Queen of Elfland laughed again. 'Now you are mine, Thomas,' she said. 'And you must come with me and serve me for seven years, through weal or woe, or whatever may chance to happen.'

And so, up with her into the saddle again, light as a blown feather, and bidding Thomas get up behind her. And willy nilly, Thomas must obey: though it seemed he was not unwilling.

Away they rode, away and away. The silver bells rang out a merry chime, and the horse galloped faster than any wind that blows. Away and away and far away, right out of the land of the living, and came at last to a vast desert where no man had ever been.

And on the edge of that desert the Queen of Elfland slid from her horse and sat down; and bid Thomas come and lay his head upon her knees.

'Now Thomas,' said she, 'keep quite still, and I will show you three marvellous sights.'

So Thomas kept quite still, with his head on her knees. At first he saw only the desert, stretching away flat and dreary into the far distance. And then, as he looked, something took shape in the desert. It was a long, long, narrow stony road, thicketed with thorns and briars; and in some places the thorns spread right across the road and choked it, so that it seemed there could be no passing.

And the Queen of Elfland said, 'Do you know what that road is, Thomas? That is the Path of Righteousness, but there are very few who seek to travel along it. So now, look again, Thomas.'

Thomas looked. The narrow stony road disappeared. And there across the desert lay a broad, broad, smooth road, bordered by lilies.

And the Queen of Elfland said, 'What you see now, Thomas, is the Path of Wickedness; though there are some folk who call it the Road to Heaven. But neither of those roads is the road that we shall go, Thomas. So look again.'

Thomas looked. The broad, smooth road disappeared.

Said the Queen of Elfland, 'What do you see now, Thomas?'

83

'Oh,' cried Thomas, 'I see a bonny, bonny road, neither narrow nor broad, neither smooth nor stony: a bonny, bonny road that winds in and out through banks of fern. That is the road for me!'

'And that is the road we must go,' said she, 'for that is the road that leads to fair Elfland. But Thomas, when we get to Elfland you must hold your tongue, whatever you may hear or see. For he who speaks a word in Elfland will never win home again.'

Then the Queen of Elfland was up on her horse again, and Thomas was up behind her, and on they galloped, and on and on, till the sun went down, and daylight faded, and darkness fell: a thick, thick darkness with not the glimpse of a moon nor the glimmer of a star, a darkness in which Thomas could see nothing at all. But he knew they were wading through swirling rivers, for the water was slapping against the horse's knees: and far off Thomas could hear the roaring of the sea.

Now they were wading through something else, something thick and warm. What was it, Thomas wondered.

And the Queen of Elfland read his thoughts and said, 'It's blood, Thomas. Every drop of blood you men shed on earth flows through the springs of this country. It flows and flows and goes on flowing. So it has always been, so it will always be, until men cease to shed it.'

On they rode, and on, and farther on, the silver bells chiming and the horse going swifter than any wind. And they left the dark, dark night behind them, and came to a garden, sparkling with morning dew and gay with flowers. At the end of the garden was an orchard; and the Queen of Elfland lighted down, and went into the orchard and plucked an apple from one of the trees.

'Take this for your wages, true Thomas,' she said. 'Eat this apple, and it will give you a tongue that can never lie.'

'*What!*' cried Thomas. 'A fine gift you would give me! My tongue is my own, to speak lies or truth as I please! If I am to speak nothing but the truth, how can I buy or sell in any market? If my tongue can never lie, how can I speak to those who think themselves above me—the princelings and lords of the world? If

I may not speak a few false flatteries, how can I ever ask a favour of a fair lady?'

But the Queen of Elfland laughed and bid him hold his tongue. It must be as she said. And Thomas had to eat that apple.

And so at last they came to Elfland, and Thomas got a fine new coat and a pair of green velvet shoes. And he stayed in Elfland for seven years: but what he did there, or what he saw, no man knows, for Thomas would never speak of it.

And at the end of the seven years the Queen brought him again on her milk-white steed to Huntley Bank, and there she left him. But before she went she told him that he must return to her whenever she sent for him. And she gave him a gift, too: the gift of foretelling future happenings.

Thomas went back to his home in the village of Ercildowne, and lived for a long time in honour and happiness. He became famous for his soothsayings; and great lords, as well as humble folk, came to consult him about the future. What he told them would happen, always did happen. Of course it did! Because his tongue could speak no lie.

And then one day, as he was making merry with some friends, a man came running in to where they sat. The man was staring and stuttering.

'A hart and a hind have come out of the forest!' he cried. 'The creatures are white as snow, their horns are golden, and they are walking up and down the village street as if they were looking for something. What does it mean, Thomas?'

'Yes, tell us what it means, Soothsayer!' cried Thomas's merry companions.

'It means that I must leave you,' said Thomas quietly.

And he got up and went out. And when the hart and hind saw him, they turned and walked back into the forest. And Thomas went into the forest after them.

Nor was he ever seen again.

THE HEIR OF LINNE

WILLIE, the Lord of Linne's son, was a careless lad, and every penny that came his way he spent. He had gay companions enough, you may be sure, to help him squander his money. His father rebuked him, his mother scolded him: Willie took no heed. He spent, and he spent, and he went on spending. 'I am the Heir of Linne,' said he to himself, 'all this great estate will one day be mine—so why shouldn't I have a little fun?'

And then his father died, and his mother died. And when she was dying, Willie's mother gave him a little golden key on a silver chain and said, 'My son, wear this round your neck for my sake. Keep it until you are in most need, for I fear you will come to need, Willie. So give me your promise that you will never part with this key, that I may die happy.'

And Willie promised.

After both his parents were dead, Willie sorrowed for a while —he wasn't a bad lad at heart. But he was now Lord of Linne; all the great estate of Linne, with its castle and its farms and its acres, was now his, and when he thought of that, he cheered up, summoned his boon companions and lived merrily again. And he spent, and he spent, and he went on spending, till all his gold was gone.

So one day, when he was sitting drearily enough in his great castle, wondering what he could do to get some more money, a man called John of Scales came to see him. And John of Scales was carrying a heavy bag.

Said John of Scales, 'How does it fare with you, my Lord of Linne?'

Said Willie, Lord of Linne, 'It fares so badly, it couldn't fare worse. I have no money left.'

86

Said John of Scales, 'Then sell me your castle and your lands, and you shall have gold in plenty. Come, I'm a good fellow, I will pay you fairly in gold, and I will pay you now. See, here's the God's penny!'

And he threw down a penny on the table, as was the custom in those days to bind a bargain.

Willie was delighted. There and then he agreed to sell his inheritance.

John of Scales opened his heavy bag, and onto the table he poured out gold and more gold. 'Come take up your money, and get you gone,' said he, 'for I am now Lord of Linne.'

Willie took the money and went off merrily enough. 'Now here is gold in plenty,' said he, 'for me and all my friends. We can eat and drink and dance and play!'

So Willie spent, and spent, and went on spending; and he and his companions lived riotously for three quarters of a year. And then there came a day when—oh horror!—Willie looked into his money chest and found it empty. Yes, he was without a penny in the world!

And Willie said to his merry companions, 'Lads, you have shared my wealth whilst it lasted; now I must look to you.' But his merry companions answered, 'To the devil with you, you feckless fellow!' And off they went to dance attendance on John of Scales, the new Lord of Linne.

Ah, well-a-day, the one-time Heir of Linne must now sell his gay clothes and his rings and diamond pins and jewelled shoe-buckles for bread. But he didn't sell the little golden key that hung round his neck on its silver chain: he had promised his mother that he wouldn't part with it, and he kept his promise. So, when he had no more gay clothes, or rings, or diamond pins, or shoe-buckles to sell, he went forth to beg, carrying with him three bags to hold whatever people would give him.

Some gave him crusts of bread, some gave him none. Some mocked at his rags. Some set the dogs on him. Some cursed him for a thriftless lout and bid him go get work. But Willie didn't know how to work, and he became more and more ragged and miserable.

One day, weary and footsore, he passed by a little house, and there was his old nurse singing at the window. And Willie stood at the corner of the house to listen, and the tears ran down his cheeks.

So he stepped out from the corner of the house and stood under the window. 'Sing that song over again, my nurse,' said he, 'for it minds me that I was once happy.'

But his nurse ran to open her door, and said, 'Come in, my bairn, and rest yourself with me! Alas, alas, that I should see you come to this! I who have seen you in better days among grand company!'

And he went in and said, 'I pray you give me a slice of your bread, nurse, and a bottle of your wine. And I will pay you back a thousandfold when I am once more Lord of Linne.'

'You'll get a slice of bread,' said she, 'and a bottle of my wine. But you'll pay me when the seas go dry, my bairn, for you'll never more be Lord of Linne.'

She begged him to stay with her, but no, he wouldn't: he was ashamed to batten on an old woman's savings. He ate and drank, and then he went out to wander again. Oh but he was weary of his life! What could he do? He would go and have a last look at Castle Linne, and then he would lie down and die.

So off with him, a long, long way, through the great park of Linne, till he came to the castle and stood at the door. And from within he heard men's laughter, and shouts of merriment, and loud singing: and he went in, for there was no one at the door to say him nay. And so he came into the great hall, and there he saw John of Scales, the new Lord of Linne, and his wife the Lady of Linne, sitting to dine. And round the table sat all Willie's old companions, eating and drinking and making merry at John of Scales's expense, just as they had at Willie's expense in former days.

And Willie went round the table with his begging bags.

'Will you give me a sup of wine and a morsel of meat, John of Scales, for when I had much I gave you more than that.'

'Ha! ha! ha! Pass round the cup, give the poor beggar a sup!' roared John of Scales; and he splashed wine into Willie's face.

'Ha! ha! ha! Give the poor beggar a bone!' yelled one of Willie's old companions. 'Here you are, your worship, Heir of

Linne! You can gnaw that as you go on your way!' And he tossed a bone at Willie and struck him on the head.

'Ha! ha! ha! Give him a fish fin! Give him a chicken bone! Let him lap up spilled gravy from the floor!'

How they laughed, how they jeered to see him standing there, so ragged and so humble.

But there was one young fellow at the table who felt ashamed, and he put his hand in his pocket and took out forty pence. 'Willie,' said he, 'it grieves me sore to see you come to this; for you were once as sprightly a boy as ever walked in Linne. Here lad, take this, and get yourself a meal.'

And he gave Willie the forty pence.

And Willie stood up beside John of Scales's wife, and said, 'Dame, my feet are weary with walking. I can stand no longer. Will you not give me a little corner where I may sit and rest?'

'Sit and rest!' cried she. 'No beggar sits to rest in this company! Go, get you gone! The street is the place for beggars. And in the street you can sit on the causeway, if your feet won't let you stand!'

So Willie went out and wandered drearily around the great castle, looking up at the walls and the towers that had once been his own. And he thought of his father and his mother: and then he remembered how his mother had given him the little golden key that still hung round his neck. What had his mother said? 'Keep it until you are in most need.'

'And by my faith,' thought he, 'I shall never be in more need than I am now!'

And he unfastened the key from its silver chain, and held it in his hand, and looked at it.

Such a little key must surely fit a little lock; and a little lock might open a little door. But what little door? And where should he find it? Outside the castle? Inside the castle? He walked all round the castle, but he found no little door. So he went into the castle again, and passed through the great hall. The wine was still flowing, and the rafters echoed with songs and drunken laughter. Willie kept close against the wall, but John of Scales saw him and shouted, 'What, ragamuffin, not gone yet? Didn't I tell you to take yourself off?'

'I am taking myself off,' said Willie.

And he passed through the hall and went up the great stairway, and into room after room. Some rooms he remembered well, some he had forgotten; and still he was searching for a door with a lock that the little key would fit. But the doors were huge and heavy, and the locks were big, and the keys that stood in them were massive.

And Willie went along and along passages, and up and up stairways, till he came to the garrets, musty, dusty, and unused. And in the very last garret he came to—yes, there was a little door under the sloping wall. And, yes, the little golden key fitted the lock of that little door: and Willie turned the key and opened the door.

And inside the door was a big cupboard, and on the cupboard floor stood three huge chests. Willie lifted the lid of one chest—what did he see? The chest was full, full of gold coins. He lifted the lid of the second chest—what did he see? That chest, too, was full, full of gold coins. He lifted the lid of the third chest—what did he see? The chest was full, full of silver coins.

And Willie fell on his knees, and wept, and blessed his mother. Then swiftly he filled up all three of his begging bags with gold coins, and yet he left far more in those chests than he took out of them. And so down the stairs and along the passages and down the stairs again as fast as he could go, and came back into the great hall.

He marched boldly up to John of Scales and said, 'I'll take a cup of wine with you now, my new-found lord. And I think you might ask me to sit down!'

'Sit down!' jeered John of Scales. 'And why should a beggar sit down? To be sure I'd give a seat to the *Heir of Linne*, if so be that he were here. How fares it with you now, my sometime *Heir of Linne*? Are you longing to possess your lands again. Will you buy them back from me, my ragged lord? By heaven, I'll sell them to you for twenty pounds less than ever I bought them from you! ha, ha, ha! You've only to throw down a penny, you know, my bonny *Heir of Linne*, only one penny to bind the bargain! And surely you can spare a penny, my sometime *Heir of Linne*, for I saw a foolish fellow that gave you forty pence a while ago.'

'I take you at your word, John of Scales,' said Willie.

And he threw down a penny onto John of Scales's plate.

'I call all present,' cried he, 'to witness what John of Scales has said!'

'Ha, ha! Ha, ha!' John of Scales laughed till he all but choked. 'The bargain's struck, Willie, the bargain's struck! But where is the gold, Willie, to buy back your lands from me? For thirty-nine pence won't buy them back, Willie, and I think that's all you now have!'

'The gold is here, John of Scales!' cried Willie. And he opened his begging bags and poured out gold upon the table. 'The lands are mine, and the gold is yours, John of Scales!' he shouted. 'But you are no longer Lord of Linne, that title belongs to me!'

Old and young leaped shouting from their seats, and crowded round to count the money. John of Scales stared and John of Scales muttered. He wanted to say that it was all his joke, but the company shouted him down. He had accepted the God's penny, and the deal was binding. Ah, he looked foolish now, did John of Scales. And John of Scales's wife wrung her hands and wept.

'Woe's me! Woe's me!' she cried. 'Yesterday I was Lady of Linne, and now I'm a nobody! And if that isn't sorrow enough, my stupid old husband has lost us twenty pounds! Eh Willie, my lad, you might as well hand over that twenty pounds! What's twenty pounds to you, with all your store of gold?'

Ho, indeed! Might he hand over that twenty pounds? Not Willie! He wasn't having any nonsense from the woman who had refused to let him sit down. John of Scales got not one penny more than the sum he had named. But Willie counted out forty pounds and handed them to the lad who had given him forty pence. 'For you are a good fellow,' said he 'and if you will, you shall be keeper of my forests. But as for you, John of Scales, get you gone out of my castle, and never trespass here again!'

So John of Scales took himself off, and his weeping wife went after him. And Willie sent the lad who had given him forty pence running to fetch his nurse. And when she came, he laughed and said, 'Nurse, the seas still ebb and flow. It will be long before they run dry! But all the same I will pay you for my bread and wine, for now I am once more the Lord of Linne.'

'The Lord of Linne! The Lord of Linne!' The company cheered and shouted. All Willie's old boon companions were ready now to lick his boots. Aha! Now they would help him once again to squander his gold, as they did in the good old days! But Willie had learned his lesson. He had his estate back, and he meant to keep it.

So he bid them all go hang, and drove them from his door. 'And may the fiend fly away with me,' said he, 'if ever I put my lands in jeopardy again for the likes of you!'

THE LOCHMABEN HARPER

THERE WAS ONCE A HARPER who lived in Lochmaben, and he was blind. Well, well, what a silly, simple old fellow he seemed! But he wasn't as silly or as simple as folk thought—no, not by a long way.

So one day he said to his wife, 'Woman, I'm off to Carlisle town.'

Says she, 'And what for?'

Says he, 'Oh, nothing much. Just to get King Henry's horse, the handsome one he calls Wanton Brown. I could do with that handsome horse, so I could!'

'You'll never manage to get it,' says she.

'Oh yes I will,' says he. 'All I need is a mare with a foal.'

'Well, you've got that,' says she. 'There's your own good grey one, and the bonny tiny foal that runs beside her.'

Says he, 'I'll leave the bonny tiny foal home with you, and get me up on the good grey mare.'

So they brought the foal inside their gate, and the harper got up on the grey mare's back, and off with him to Carlisle. He knew the road all right; you'd think he had seeing eyes instead of blind ones, the way he managed to get about.

And when he came to the gate of Carlisle castle, who should be standing there but King Henry.

'Come in, come in, you silly blind harper,' says King Henry. 'Come into my hall, and let me hear your harping.'

'Oh truly, so you shall,' says the silly blind harper. 'But first give me stabling for my mare.'

So the king called his stable groom and said, 'Go take the silly blind harper's mare and tie her up beside Wanton Brown.'

The stable groom did that. And the harper went into the king's hall.

He harped and he harped and he harped; and he sang and he sang and he sang. And so merry were his tunes that all the lords and ladies in the hall got up and danced. And King Henry dancing with the best of them.

And when King Henry and the lords and ladies were tired out with their dancing, what did that silly blind harper do? He went on harping, and he went on singing, but now his tunes and songs were sad, sad and sleepy ones. King Henry yawned, the ladies yawned, the lords yawned; their heads nodded, their eyes blinked, they settled down on the floor and the benches and all fell fast asleep.

Then the silly blind harper took off his shoes; he crept quietly down the stairs; with tread as light as light could be, he stole across the yard to the stable door. Ha! ha! though he was blind he could find his way about! Into the stable he goes, and there in their stalls stood thirty-three horses. But the silly blind harper knew his grey mare among them all, and next to her stood the king's Wanton Brown. And that silly blind harper had a colt halter tucked away in his breeches.

So what does he do? He takes the halter out of his breeches, slips it over the Wanton's head, and ties the end of the halter rope to his grey mare's tail. He leads his grey mare out of the

94

stable, and Wanton Brown, being tied to her, must follow at her tail. He leads the grey mare to the castle gates, opens the gates, and lets her go.

See! She's off like a shot arrow—she has a foal back at Lochmaben, hasn't she? And she has but one thought in her head—to get back to that foal. Off with her then, galloping, galloping, over moor and moss, over hill and valley—off with her, galloping, galloping, and Wanton Brown kicking up his heels and galloping after her, fast tied to her tail.

The mare goes so fast that she reaches Lochmaben gate full three hours before daylight; and there she stands, snorting and whinnying.

The silly blind harper's wife woke and heard her. Says she to her serving maid, 'Get up, get up, you lazy lass! Go to the gate and let in your master and his mare.'

The maid got up, put on her clothes, and went yawning to the gate. She took the key out of the lock and peeped through the keyhole. 'Oh lor!' cried she, and 'oh lor!' cried she, 'our mare has got a fine brown foal!'

Her mistress got up and hurried to the gate. 'Come hold your tongue, you foolish lass!' said she. 'It's but the moonlight dazzling your eyes. I'll wager all I've got against a penny that the animal out there at the mare's tail is bigger than any foal of ours could be!'

And she opened the gate, brought the mare to her foal, gave Wanton Brown a good feed and tied him up in the stable.

'But what your master's doing with himself this night,' says she to the girl, 'is more than I or anyone else can tell.'

The silly blind harper had gone back into the king's hall. He put on his shoes and began to harp and sing once more. The ladies woke, the lords woke, King Henry woke: but bless me so sweetly and merrily the harper harped, and so gaily he sang, that they thought of nothing but to stay where they were, and listen to him.

But with the dawn of day in rushed the stable groom shouting, 'The Wanton Brown is stolen away, and so is the silly blind harper's mare!'

'Alas! Alas!' cried the silly blind harper. 'Is this the way I'm

95

paid for pleasuring you? In Scotland I lost a bonny colt-foal; in England they've stolen my good grey mare!'

'Come, cease your "alasing",' said the king. 'You shall be well paid for your colt-foal, and I will give you a far better mare.'

So the silly blind harper went back into the hall and harped and sang. And the lords and ladies, as they sat at breakfast, all agreed that never had they heard such sweet harping or such merry singing.

And the silly blind harper chuckled to himself. The king paid him handsomely for the foal he'd never lost, and three times the value of the good grey mare. And when that silly blind harper went back to Lochmaben, he was riding on the best mare of all the mares in the king's stable.

'A merry night's work,' thinks he to himself. 'And may there be more as merry!'

KING ORFEO

KING ORFEO had a harp with which he made music such as
the world had never heard before. When he played the birds of
the air and the wild beasts of the forest would gather about him
to listen; and all men who heard his music must sing or weep or
dance, according to his will. Truly, King Orfeo loved his harp.
But greater than his love for his harp was his love for his
beautiful queen, whose name was Isabel.

Now one May morning Queen Isabel went out with two of
her maidens to walk in the garden. The sun was bright, the air
was sweet, the little birds sang merrily. Queen Isabel sat down
under an apple tree to listen to the birds. And from listening she
got to drowsing, and from drowsing to sleeping: until there she
was, stretched out under the apple tree, sound, sound asleep.

The two maidens strolled about the garden, stooped to smell
the flowers, talked in low voices: not for the world would they
disturb their sleeping queen. Now and then they tiptoed to
where she lay, to assure themselves that all was well with her.
Yes, she slept on, sweetly, peacefully.

'How lovely is our queen!' whispered one maiden to the other
maiden. 'Surely heaven and earth and all that is under the earth
must envy King Orfeo his beautiful wife!'

Just then a big bright butterfly flew past on gold and purple
wings, and the maidens ran to follow the butterfly as it flitted
about the garden. The butterfly settled on a flower, its gorgeous
wings outspread: but even as the maidens tiptoed close to
admire it, they heard a terrible scream. . . .

It was their queen screaming!

Oh what was the matter, what was the matter? The maidens

97

ran to the apple tree: their queen was sitting up, her face was deadly pale, her eyes wild with terror, her mouth wide open, uttering scream after scream. The maidens flung their arms round her, but she pushed them off, leaped up, tore her clothes, tore her beautiful golden hair. The maidens ran to the palace, 'Help! Help! Our queen has gone mad!'

Knights and ladies—a great company—rushed into the garden. The knights caught up the struggling queen, carried her into the palace, the ladies put her to bed. King Orfeo ran to her, took her in his arms, 'My queen, my queen, tell me what ails you! Tell me, only tell me, what I can do to comfort you!'

And in the king's arms the queen grew calmer. She was not screaming or struggling any more; but only sobbing, sobbing.

'Oh my lord and king,' she sobbed, 'I have loved you more than life, but now we two must part!'

'Whilst I live nothing shall part you from me!' cried King Orfeo.

But the sobbing queen told him that whilst she slept an unearthly knight came to her and bid her go with him to his king. And when she said she would not go with him, he laughed and went away. And then there came a great company of lords and ladies riding on snow-white steeds, and in their midst rode a king with a starry crown. And the king with the starry crown lifted her in his arms and set her on his snow-white steed, and carried her away to where his castle stood, all silver shining in a soft glow of milky light.

'This is where you will dwell henceforth,' said the king with the starry crown. 'Prepare yourself to come to us.'

And then he carried her back to the apple tree and set her down.

'See that tomorrow noon you are waiting under this tree,' said he, 'ready to go with us. And if we do not find you waiting, we will come and take you by force, wherever you may be.'

'And I know he will come,' sobbed Queen Isabel, 'and I know he will carry me away. And oh, my dearest lord and king, I feel mad with grief and fear!'

But King Orfeo told her again and again that no king in heaven or on earth or under the earth should take her from

98

him. And he held her in his arms until she ceased to weep. All that day, and all through the night, King Orfeo held his queen in his arms. And next day, when it drew towards noon, he summoned a thousand knights, took his queen to the apple tree, and waited with her there, surrounded by his thousand knights.

'We will let no one take away our queen,' said he to his thousand knights.

And the leader of the thousand knights answered, 'We are resolved to die, if need be, in her defence. We will give her up to no one in heaven or on earth or under the earth.'

And they waited. And the shadow on the sundial moved slowly, slowly, until it pointed to twelve, noon.

King Orfeo was holding the queen's hand in his, he was looking into her lovely eyes, and those lovely eyes looked back into his. And suddenly, as the shadow of the dial pointed to noon, those lovely eyes grew dim, faded, vanished. Where they had been was nothing but the moving shadows of the leaves; and where the queen's hand had lain clasped in King Orfeo's hand, there was nothing, nothing, nothing! The king's hand clutched but empty air. The queen had vanished.

And the king all but died of grief. . . .

But what avail to die of grief? Nay, he would live, and set out to find his queen and rescue her, wherever she might be. So he gave his kingdom into the charge of his high steward, told his barons that if they should at any time hear of his death, they should choose a new king to rule over them, laid his crown on the altar in his chapel, knelt to say a prayer for his dear queen and himself, took off his royal robes, dressed himself in a coarse woollen garment, took his harp in his hand, and walked barefoot out of his palace gates to wander through the world.

For ten years King Orfeo wandered, seeking, seeking. His body wasted away, his beard grew down to his girdle; his only comfort was his harp. And sometimes, when the sunlight shone brightly on some barren heath, or flickered among the leaves of some wild wood, King Orfeo would make his harp play marvellously of his searching and his sorrow. Then the birds of the heath, and the wild beasts of the woodland would gather about

99

him to listen; and the beasts would rub their soft furry bodies against him, bidding him not despair; and the birds would chirrup hope into his ears. And he would get up and wander on, searching, searching.

And sometimes he heard strange sounds and saw strange sights. He heard the ringing of bridle chains, and over the heath or through the woods, a fairy host would come riding by on snow-white steeds; and in their midst rode the king with the starry crown. And King Orfeo would cry out to them, and run to follow where they went: but always they vanished again, and left him desolate. And sometimes, on wide grassy places, he would see knights and ladies dancing in a ring, and he would go to where they danced: and behold, there was nothing to see but the deep green ring left on the sward by their dancing feet. And so he wandered on and on, through ten long years.

And after those ten years had passed, he came to a wild country of rocks and bushes, and saw, coming towards him, a company of ladies dressed in white, and riding on snow-white steeds. The ladies carried white hawks on their wrists, and before and behind them ran a pack of snow-white hounds.

The company came nearer and nearer: fifty-nine ladies passed him by with never a look; but the last, the sixtieth turned her head and gazed into his eyes. It was his queen! She held out her arms to him, he held out his arms to her. . . . but alas, alas, another rider caught her bridle and hurried her along; but still she turned her head and gazed at him; and the tears ran down her cheeks.

'My queen! My queen!' No, those riders should *not* escape him, hurry as they might! King Orfeo ran as he had never run in his life: stumbling over huge stones, tripped up by bushes, he ran, ran, ran. And though the riders galloped, he kept them in sight: saw them, far ahead, come to a great grey rock, saw the rock open, saw the whole company—riders, hawks, hounds and all—pass in through the rock and disappear.

Panting, hot, shaken by a wild rage, King Orfeo reached the rock and struck it with his fist. 'Open, open!' he cried. 'Open, stubborn rock! You shall not part me from my queen!'

And lo! the rock opened, and within it was a long passage,

going down, down, down into the earth: a passage grey and twilit as a place of dream.

King Orfeo stopped neither to take breath nor think; along that passage he ran, along, and along, and down, down, down. Faint and far off he could hear the soft trampling of hoofs, and now and then the baying of a hound. And so at last he came to the end of the passage, and saw before him a flowery meadow, and beyond the meadow a castle, palely glimmering, as if lit by moonbeams.

The castle gates were open, for the company of riders was just passing through; but by the time King Orfeo reached those gates, they were closed again. And there he stood, knocking, knocking at the gates for hours it seemed to him: and the castle rang with the echoes, and no one came.

But at last the gates slowly opened, and a pale porter looked out.

'Who are you?' said the porter. 'And what is your errand here?'

'I am a minstrel,' said King Orfeo, 'come to play before your king.'

And the porter let him in.

King Orfeo then passed through a garden, and in the garden was an apple tree, and under the apple tree his queen lay fast asleep. But try as he would, King Orfeo could not approach that apple tree, so thick was the magic spread around it. So he hurried on, and came to the great door of the palace, and went through and into an immense hall. Ladies and knights thronged the hall, and on a diamond throne sat the king who wore the starry crown.

King Orfeo went up to the throne and knelt before it.

'What man are you?' said he of the starry crown. 'I never sent for you. And never before have I found a man so bold as to come here unbidden.'

'Lord,' said King Orfeo, 'I am but a poor minstrel; and it is the manner of minstrels to seek the palaces of kings, even though they be not welcome.'

'Let me hear your music,' said he of the starry crown.

And King Orfeo ran his fingers over his harp strings, and began to play.

Ah, what music! Such music as had never been heard in that hall before: sad music that would make the whole world weep; happy music that would make the whole world laugh; merry music that would make the whole world dance; tender, loving music that would make the sick man rise smiling from his bed, to say 'Lo, I am healed!'

The king with the starry crown leaned from his throne to listen; the knights and the ladies clustered about King Orfeo; they sat at his feet, they wept, they laughed, they leaped up and danced: what the harp music bid them do, they did. And King Orfeo played on and on.

Until at last the king with the starry crown stepped down from his throne, and bid King Orfeo cease. 'For you have laid a spell upon my people, stronger than any spell in the Land of Fairy,' he said, 'and that I cannot permit. So go your way out of my kingdom, minstrel; but before you go, ask what you will, and I promise I will grant your request.'

'Lord,' said King Orfeo, 'give me the lady who sleeps under the apple tree.'

'Nay, minstrel, nay!' said he of the starry crown. 'Think what you ask, and ask more wisely! You are lean and worn and ragged, scorched by a thousand suns, drenched by a thousand rains, bitten by a thousand frosts, beaten and torn by a thousand tempests. The lady who sleeps under the apple tree is lovely as the dawn, suns may not scorch her, nor tempests beat upon her, nor cold and wet rob her of her beauty. It were a loathly thing to see her in your company.'

'Lord,' answered King Orfeo, 'more loathly than all else is a broken promise in a king's mouth.'

'Then take her and get you gone!' cried he of the starry crown, 'and never venture again into my presence!'

King Orfeo bowed low and turned to go from the hall; the company of lords and ladies stood aside to let him pass, and no one spoke a word. And when King Orfeo, blithe of heart, went out into the garden, the magic was lifted from about the apple tree, and his queen woke from her sleep, and ran to meet him. And he ran to her and took her in his arms.

'My king!'

'My queen!'

It was nothing to either of them that he was lean and worn and ragged: hand in hand they passed out of the Land of Fairy, and went back to their own kingdom, though it was a long and weary way they went before they reached it.

And when they drew near their own palace, King Orfeo said, 'Rest you here on this grassy bank, my queen, and I will go in, and prove the hearts of my people, whether they be true or false.' And he went into the castle as a minstrel—a lean, ragged beggar—and presented himself before the high steward to whom he had given his kingdom in charge.

And though in this lean, ragged beggar the high steward did not recognize King Orfeo, yet he bade him welcome. 'Every minstrel is thrice welcome here,' he said, 'for the sake of our beloved king, whose harping was such that men must weep, or sing, or dance, according to his will.'

And King Orfeo leaned against a table in the hall and said, 'Look again, look at me hard and long, my steward, for indeed I am your king.'

Then in a wild delight the high steward gave a leap that threw over the table, fell at king Orfeo's feet, sobbed for joy, and kissed the king's ragged garment. Then up with him again, to shout the good news through the palace: and lords and ladies, barons, knights, squires and pages came running to kneel before their king. . . . But their queen, their queen, what of their lovely queen?

And King Orfeo led them to where the queen was waiting, and they brought her in to the triumphant fanfare of trumpets and singing and huzzaing. Now nothing would satisfy them but that King Orfeo and the queen must be crowned anew.

'For we have mourned you as dead, and you have come back to us alive!' they said.

So they held a second coronation, and feasted for twenty days and twenty nights; and throughout King Orfeo's kingdom the people danced and sang, and bonfires blazed and fountains ran with wine.

And King Orfeo, shorn of his ragged beard and dressed in his royal robes, soon lost his haggard looks and became strong and handsome again. And with his lovely queen he lived and reigned long and happily.

A TALE OF ROBIN HOOD

Part 1. The Birth of Robin Hood

NOW THEN, here's Willie, tall, strong, handsome as handsome, and come of a noble family. But Willie hasn't a penny to bless himself, with, so he goes and takes service with Earl Richard.

And here's Earl Richard's only daughter, lovely as any lily-flower—so what happens? Willie falls deeply in love with Earl Richard's daughter, and she falls as deeply in love with him. They plight their troth, they take each other for man and wife, but it must all be done in secret. No one must know, least of all Earl Richard, for he thinks his daughter should marry some duke or other, and he looks upon Willie as a mere servant. Moreover, Earl Richard has a hot and hasty temper: should he find out about those two, he wouldn't stop to eat or drink before he'd have Willie dangling from a rope over the castle wall.

But the time comes when those two can keep their secret no longer, because Earl Richard's daughter is going to have a baby. What to do now? They meet on a summer night in a copse outside the castle, and make plans to run away.

So next evening, when all was quiet, when the sun had gone down in the west, and a half moon was rising in the east, Willie went to stand under his lady's window. She opened the window and looked down. There he was, stretching up his arms, and holding out a thick robe of red scarlet cloth. So she gave a jump out of the window, and Willie caught her in the robe and wrapped it round her, and away with them both into the forest.

And that very night, under the green leaves of the forest, Willie's lady gave birth to a beautiful baby boy.

That same night Earl Richard had a bad dream. He dreamed that he saw his daughter drowning in the sea, and that he couldn't come at her to save her. So when he woke in the morning, the very first thing he did was to bid his servants fetch his daughter to him. But of course they couldn't find her. So then Earl Richard flew into one of his rages, and swore that if his daughter were sick, or if she were dead, or if she were stolen away, he'd hang all his servants up in rows for the kites to pick at.

Then you may be sure there was a running up and down stairs, a ransacking of all the rooms, a searching and hallooing through the castle grounds, a leaping onto horseback and a galloping all over the countryside. Had any one seen Earl Richard's daughter? No, no one had.

But at last, as some of the servants were riding slowly through the forest, all unwilling to return to Earl Richard, lest he carry out his threat and hang them—what did they see? There, happy as you please, sitting on the mossy ground, with her back against an oak tree, was Earl Richard's daughter, with her baby boy in her arms.

So off galloped the servants back to Earl Richard with the joyful news. Now it was Earl Richard himself who galloped off to the forest. Now it was only Willie that Earl Richard was going to hang!

But when he came to where his daughter sat, there was no sight of Willie. There was only his beloved daughter with the baby in her arms. And at the sight of that baby, Earl Richard's heart melted:

'My grandson! My bonny little grandson!'

He forgave his daughter then and there; for indeed she was very dear to him. He took the baby up in his arms, kissed him again and again. 'Robin Hood in good greenwood!' he cried. 'Robin Hood shall be your name!'

And he took his daughter and the baby home.

And though we are not told what became of Willie, it seems that Earl Richard forgot all about wanting to hang him.

So Robin Hood grew up in his grandfather's castle. But he had been born in the greenwood, and the greenwood called him back. Nothing pleased him so much as to be out in the forest with his bow and arrows, shooting the deer. Now all the deer

in England belonged to the king, and the penalty for shooting them without permission was death. That is, if you were caught; and if you were not caught, you became an outlaw. Much Robin cared! He was proud and spirited, and gay, and generous; he would live his own life, king or no king! So, when he was about twenty years old, he got him a green jerkin and a green hood, took his bow and arrows, and went to live in the greenwood. And soon he gathered about him a company of merry young men, all bold and high-spirited, and all outlaws like himself.

But how, you may well ask, did Robin and his merry men manage to live in the greenwood? Of course they shot the king's deer for meat; but they needed more than meat, they needed bread and wine and clothes and weapons: and all these things cost money. How did they get that money? Well, they got it by robbery. But Robin had his own notions about whom they should rob and whom they shouldn't; and calling his merry men to the trysting tree, which was the place where they met and kept their weapons, he gave them these orders:

'You shall rob no honest farmer; you shall rob no good knight, nor squire, nor poor labourer, nor wandering minstrel. All these people you shall help in any way you can; and to whomsoever you find in need you shall give with both hands full, nor count the cost.

'But fat, lazy monks, and insolent abbots and bishops and archbishops, and the rich and idle and proud and wicked— these shall be your prey.

'Take from the rich and greedy, give to the poor and needy. And what is over, when we have done our alms, shall be ours to keep. This shall be our rule, my merry men all, and in this way we shall do well enough.'

And indeed they did do well: Robin became richer than many a landed lord. And though the rich and proud went in deadly fear of him, all poor and honest people loved him and wished him well.

What larks those outlaws were up to, what pranks they played, what havoc they made amongst the king's deer! The doings of Robin and his merry men were talked about all up and down

the country. The wandering minstrels in their journeyings
treasured up the stories of these doings; they made them into
ballads, and sang the ballads to earn their supper in castle and
hall. The people who gathered to listen to the minstrels, loved
to hear these songs about Robin Hood. They listened until they
knew the tunes and the words by heart; and years and years
later the words of the songs came to be written down and printed,
so that now we can all read about Robin Hood and his adven-
tures.

The minstrels sang of Robin's birth too; and this is what they
sang:

> O many one sings of grass, of grass,
> And many one sings of corn,
> And many one sings of Robin Hood
> Knows little of where he was born.
>
> It was not in the hall, the hall,
> Nor in the painted bower,
> But it was in the good greenwood
> Among the lily flower.

Little John was one of Robin's most devoted followers. His real name was John Little, but because he was such a huge fellow—well over seven feet tall—they nicknamed him Little John. Well, being such a huge fellow he had a huge appetite, and one day, when he was feeling very hungry, he said to Robin Hood, 'Master, surely it's time for dinner!'

But Robin said no: he was not going to dine until his men had brought him a guest. And that guest must be a rascally lord or a fat, greedy abbot—someone who could pay well for what he ate. For it was Robin's little joke to dine at the expense of such people.

So off went Little John, with two others, William Scarlet and Much, to find such a guest to dine with them.

They looked east and they looked west, but no rich rascally lord or fat greedy abbot could they meet with. They were about to return to Robin and tell him he must do without a guest that day, when they saw, in a lonely place on the borders of the greenwood, a knight riding along the way.

And if ever a man looked woebegone, it was that knight. His clothes were poor and thin, his hood hung over his eyes, he had but one foot in the stirrup, and the other leg hung loose, as if he didn't care how soon he tumbled from his horse. And the horse itself was not in much better shape than its rider, being lean and rough-coated, stumbling along in its shabby trappings with its head hung down, as if it had no mind to walk another step.

'I think this knight must be our guest, for want of a better,' said Little John. And he ran up to the knight and went down on one knee.

'Welcome to the greenwood, Sir Knight!' said he. 'My master has awaited you fasting these three hours.'

'Who is your master?' said the knight.

'Sir, he is Robin Hood.'

'I have heard tell of him,' said the knight, 'how good and generous he is to those in trouble. Yes, I will go with you. Lead on, and I will follow.'

So Little John and Much and Scarlet led the way back to the trysting tree, and the knight rode behind them. He was heaving great sighs, and now and then a tear trickled down his cheek.

And so they brought him to Robin. And when Robin saw him, he took off his hood, and bowed low.

'Welcome, Sir Knight!' said Robin. 'You are more than welcome! For I have been waiting a long, long time for a guest to dine with me.'

Then, whilst some of Robin's men hurried to set out dinner on the greensward, Much took charge of the knight's horse, rubbed it down and gave it a good feed. And Little John brought a bowl of water and a towel, and Robin and the knight washed and dried their hands. And then they all sat down to dinner.

What a dinner! Venison and roasted swans, and wild fowl and turkeys done to a turn, and white bread and brimming bowls of wine and ale.

'Sir Knight,' said Robin, 'may I know your name?'

And the knight sighed and answered, 'Men call me Sir Richard at the Lee. But how much longer I may bear that name, I cannot tell.'

'Then Sir Richard at the Lee, whilst that name is still yours, I pray you do gladly!' said Robin.

And if Sir Richard did not do gladly, he at least did heartily: he ate like a starved man, and when he had eaten his fill, he said, 'I thank you from my heart, Robin Hood. I haven't had such a meal as this for the past month or more. And if it is ever in my power, though alas that is not likely, I will serve you with as good a dinner as you have now given me.'

'That is well spoken, Sir Knight,' said Robin. 'But before we part, I have a word to say. Now you have fed so well, I think you will be willing to pay for your dinner? For it was never surely the custom in any country for a mere yeoman, like myself, to pay for a knight.'

'Alas!' said the knight, 'you put me to shame. I have nothing in my saddle bags worth offering you.'

'Sir Knight,' said Robin, 'tell me the truth. How much gold have you?'

'As I live,' answered the knight, 'I have no more than ten shillings.'

'If that is all you have,' said Robin, 'may the fiend fly away with me if I touch a penny of it! Little John, go, look in the knight's saddle bags.'

Little John went to where the knight's horse was munching its oats, and the saddle bags lay on the ground. Little John looked in the saddle bags, turned them upside down, shook them: sure enough, ten shillings was all the money they contained. So Little John went back to Robin Hood. 'Master,' said he, 'the knight is true enough.'

'But tell me, Sir Knight,' said Robin, 'how has this come about? I have heard tell that Sir Richard at the Lee is master of rich lands and a fair castle. What have you done with those rich lands and that fair castle? Have you trusted those who should not be trusted? Have you fallen into bad company? Have you gambled and lived riotously?'

'Heaven be my witness,' said the knight, 'I have done none of these things. I swear I have been as honest and true and good-living a knight as all my ancestors have been before me. But I have a son who should have been my heir. And when he was twenty years old he went jousting and slew a knight from Lancashire. And though it was in fair fight, and the lad was scarce to blame, the knight's family pressed hard for revenge. So to save my son's life, I paid that family four hundred pounds. I borrowed the four hundred pounds from the rich abbot of St Mary's Abbey, and tomorrow I must pay it back, or I lose my lands. Alack, alack, I have no means of paying it back by tomorrow, and the abbot will not wait.'

'What will you do then, if you lose your lands?' asked Robin.

'What will I do?' cried the knight. 'I'll cross the sea and journey to the Holy Land, and there lie down and die. But now farewell, good friends. And in all my misery I shall remember your kindness, Robin Hood.'

And the knight got up to go, and he was weeping.

'Stay, stay!' said Robin. 'Have you no friends to help you in your need?'

'Sir,' said the knight, 'before this trouble came upon me I

had friends in plenty. But now they run from me like a flock of sheep.'

'So if a man were to lend you the money,' said Robin, 'you have no one you could name who would guarantee that you would pay it back? For a man who lends money must have some assurance that he will be repaid.'

'I can name no one,' said the knight. 'No one on earth. But our dear Lady, Queen of Heaven knows—she knows me for an honest man!'

'By my faith!' cried Robin, 'you could name no one whom I would more surely trust! Go to my treasury quickly, Little John, and bring me here four hundred pounds in gold.'

So Little John ran to Robin's treasure cave, and came back with four hundred pounds, and Robin gave the money to the knight. The knight shed tears again, but now they were tears of joy. Sobbing out his thanks, he went down on his knees to Robin.

But Robin laughed and said, ' 'Tis but a loan, Sir Richard, and a loan is no great thing. A twelvemonth from today, I shall look to see you back here at my trysting tree to repay that loan. . . . But what's the matter now, Little John, that you stand there looking so glum?'

'Master,' said Little John, 'the knight's clothing is so thin it grieves me to the heart. You have clothing enough in your treasury, scarlet cloth and Lincoln green, and rich stuffs of many colours. I think there is no merchant in all merry England so rich in cloth as you.'

'Well then,' said Robin, 'you can measure out three yards of as many colours as you fancy, and give them to the knight.'

'Trust me to measure well!' cried Little John gleefully. And he strode off to the cave, and came back staggering under the weight of great bales of cloth.

Then he unrolled the bales side by side along the ground. 'Three yards of each!' said he. 'Now see me measure it. *I* need no yard stick!' And he took a run and gave three mighty leaps along the edges of the stuffs. 'One! Two! Three! And so we cut it off!'

And cut it off he did, yards and yards and yards of each colour.

114

'What devilkin's draper do you think you are?' said Much. 'Each length you are cutting off is more like thirty yards than three!'

'Little John may well give good measure, since it costs him nothing!' laughed Scarlet. 'But Master, the knight will need a good strong nag to carry home all this gear.'

'Let him have Grey Dumpling then,' said Robin, 'for he is broad-backed enough.'

'And he should have a good palfrey for himself to ride,' said Little John, 'for his own horse will carry him no farther. The poor beast must stay here with us in the greenwood till he gets his strength back again.'

'And the knight should have a pair of new boots,' said Scarlet.

'Anything else?' laughed Robin.

'Yes, a pair of gilt spurs,' said Little John, 'such as befit a knight.'

So Robin gave Sir Richard all these things. And there was Sir Richard now mounted on one of Robin's best horses, and looking a new man, all smiles and gratefulness. And though his clothing was but poor and thin, still he had Robin's Grey Dumpling by a leading rein, and Grey Dumpling was loaded with enough rich stuffs to make him twenty new suits.

'Farewell, farewell, good Robin Hood,' said he. 'Farewell until today twelvemonth, when I shall come back to pay my debt.'

He was about to ride off then, but Robin said, 'Stay, stay, Sir Richard at the Lee, you mustn't ride alone: a knight should have a squire to go behind him. Get you to horse, Little John, and squire the knight back to his castle. And mind you pay him due respect, for such is a squire's duty!'

So Little John, mounted on one of Robin's biggest horses, rode solemnly off behind Sir Richard at the Lee. It was Little John now who had Grey Dumpling by the leading rein. The knight turned his head many times to smile and wave, and call down blessings on Robin Hood and all his merry men; but Little John rode stiff and straight, looking neither to this side nor that, but keeping his eyes fixed on the knight's back—playing the part of devoted squire with a solemn face but with many inward chuckles.

And the greenwood rang with cheers from Robin and his merry men, as they watched the riders until they were out of sight.

Part 3. Sir Richard at the Lee and the Abbot

Next day Sir Richard at the Lee set off for St Mary's Abbey to pay the abbot the money he had borrowed. He was riding Robin Hood's fine horse, but he still had on his poor thin clothing. He had left his new boots and his gilt spurs at home, and all the company he had brought with him was but one young lad to hold his horse.

Inside the abbey, the abbot was gleefully rubbing his hands as he sat at dinner. He had summoned the High Justice, and the Sheriff of Nottingham and a great gathering of proud lords to feast with him and witness the disinheriting of Sir Richard.

'For the knight can never pay that four hundred pounds,' said the abbot, 'and so all his lands and his fair castle will this day be mine!'

'I dare swear he has fled overseas by this time,' said the Justice. 'He will never have the impudence to come here and plead for mercy!'

'Nay, by this time the wretched fellow will have hanged himself,' said a fat-cheeked monk who was the abbot's high cellarer. 'We shall all live the merrier when Sir Abbot gets his lands!'

And there was only one among all that company who felt sorry for Sir Richard, and that was the prior.

'The day is young,' said the prior, 'Sir Richard may yet come. And if he cannot pay, we should grant him grace, Sir Abbot, or you will have a heavy sin on your conscience. I would rather pay down a hundred pounds myself than rob a good man of his lands.'

'*Rob!*' cried the abbot. 'Who talks of robbing? The deal was fair and square, the agreement is signed, as I call all you here to witness! . . . But you must be forever thwarting me, you snivelling prior! By heaven, you may as well go and hang yourself up

116

along with Sir Richard—for the world will miss neither the one nor the other of you!'

The prior went to the window and looked out. 'I see Sir Richard at the gate,' said he. 'And as you hope for mercy, Sir Abbot, show mercy now!'

'No mercy! No mercy!' shouted the abbot. 'What is fairly mine I claim!'

And he thumped the table with his fist, and bid the prior be gone out of his sight.

Outside, the porter was opening the gate to Sir Richard. 'Welcome, Sir Knight!' said he. 'My lord abbot is at dinner, and with him a great company, all gathered in your honour—if honour we can call it! But what a fine horse you have there, Sir Knight—the best courser that I ever set eyes on! Your lad shall lead him to the abbot's stable, for I think the abbot will be glad to own him!'

'No, he shall not be led to the stable,' said Sir Richard. 'He shall wait for me here at the gate, and my lad shall hold him.'

And he walked into the abbot's hall; and there he saluted all the company, and went to kneel down before the abbot.

'Have you brought your pay?' cried the abbot. 'No, I'll be sworn you haven't! So what are you doing here?'

'Alack! Alack! Might it be to pray for time?' said the knight.

'The time is up,' said the abbot, 'you know that full well. And your lands are mine!'

Then the knight turned to the Justice. 'Good Sir Justice,' said he, 'I pray you be my friend and help me against my enemies!'

'Pooh! pooh! I hold with the abbot,' said the Justice.

The knight turned to the sheriff. 'Good Sir Sheriff, be my friend!'

'Nay, not I!' cried the sheriff.

'Then good Sir Abbot,' said the knight, 'will not *you* be my friend? Hold my lands but for a little while until I can pay you. And when I have the money it shall be yours.'

But the abbot banged his fist down on the table. 'You may get your lands from whom you can,' said he. 'You don't get them from me! Away with you out of my hall, false knight! Away and hang yourself!'

'He lies who calls me false!' cried the knight, leaping up. 'But he who lets a knight kneel so long at his feet knows nothing of good manners! By heaven, no insolent abbot shall be the heir of Sir Richard at the Lee!' And he opened a bag and shook out four hundred pounds upon the table. 'Have there your gold, Sir Abbot. Had you but shown me some courtesy, I would have paid you interest on it!'

The abbot sat and stared. Of the rich food spread before him, not a bite more could he eat. In his disappointment he all but wept. But the money was paid; he had no claim now upon all those rich lands he had so greedily coveted.

Yes, the abbot sat and stared and all but wept; but Sir Richard hurried out of the abbot's hall with never a backward look, and sang merrily as he mounted his horse and rode back to his fair castle.

At the gate of his castle, his Lady ran out to meet him.

'Be merry, be merry, my dame,' cried Sir Richard. And he jumped from his horse and took her in his arms. 'Be merry, and pray for Robin Hood! For if it had not been for his kindness, we should now be beggars, both you and I!'

And after that, Sir Richard lived happily in his castle with his good wife, and managed his affairs so well that when twelve months had passed, he had the four hundred pounds put by all ready to pay back Robin Hood.

Part 4. Little John and the Sheriff of Nottingham

After Sir Richard at the Lee had poured out the four hundred pieces of gold on the abbot's table, and had walked out of St Mary's Abbey, the abbot's guests all quickly took their leave. They had no mind to stay and face the abbot's rage and disappointment. The High Justice went home to his manor, and the sheriff summoned his attendants, who were making merry in the abbot's kitchen, and set off back to Nottingham.

Now, to reach Nottingham, the sheriff had to pass the out-skirts of Sherwood forest, and though he had never so far set eyes on Robin Hood or any of his men, he went in great fear of them, and he never travelled that way without a following of well-armed servants to protect him.

Well, it so happened that on that day Little John was out alone on the edge of the forest, practising with the long bow. And there he was, shooting at a stick he had driven into the ground as a target, when the sheriff passed along. And when the sheriff saw how Little John's arrows again and again hit that far distant target, and saw, too, what a huge, strong fellow Little John was, he thought, 'It were good to have this lad in my bodyguard.' And he rode up to Little John.

'Tell me now, my fine young man,' said he, 'what is your name, and where were you born?'

And Little John answered promptly, 'I was born in Holder-ness, and men call me Reynold Greenleaf.'

'Then tell me, Reynold Greenleaf, will you be my servant? I will give you twenty marks a year, and a good strong horse to ride on.'

'I have a master already,' said Little John, 'a very courteous knight. But if I can get leave of him—yes, I will serve you. I will come to Nottingham tonight and give you my answer.'

So the sheriff rode on to Nottingham, and Little John ran laughing to Robin Hood.

Robin thought it the best joke in the world, and agreed to let Little John go. 'And mind you serve the sheriff well!' said he.

'Faith,' laughed Little John, 'I shall be the worst servant to him that ever he had yet!'

And off he went to serve the Sheriff of Nottingham.

Now one day the sheriff went off on a visit and left 'Reynold Greenleaf' at home. And Reynold Greenleaf was hungry. So he went to the butler. 'Good sir butler,' said he, 'give me my dinner. It is too long for Reynold Greenleaf to go fasting!'

And the butler, who was a surly fellow said, 'You get nothing to eat or drink till my lord sheriff comes home.'

'Will you give me to eat and drink, or shall I crack your crown for you?' said Little John. And when Little John said that, the butler fled into the buttery and slammed and bolted the door behind him. But Little John gave the door a kick and burst it open; and he gave the butler such a rap with his huge fist as the butler never forgot to the end of his life. That rap sent the butler hurtling out through the broken-down door, nor did he venture in again. And Little John found meat in plenty and ale in plenty, and ate and drank his fill.

And he had just about finished eating when the cook came out of the kitchen, and looked in at the buttery door. The cook was a strong fellow, not so big, certainly as Little John, but well muscled and full of brawn.

'Well on my word, Reynold Greenleaf,' said the cook, 'a fine servant you are, making free of your master's victuals and asking no man's leave! Take that, you saucy knave, and that, and that!'

And the cook doubled up his fist and gave Little John three hard blows.

Little John sprang to his feet. 'Faith and I like these blows!' he cried. 'There is muscle and lustihood behind them! Come outside and draw your sword, good fellow, and we will prove now which of us is the better man!'

So each man took his sword, and they went out together into the sheriff's garden. Up and down the garden walks and among the flower beds they fought for an hour, and neither could best the other, or even give him a prick, so skilful were they both in their sword play.

And Little John was full of admiration for the cook; so

when, at the end of an hour, they paused for a breather, he said, 'Master cook, you are one of the best swordsmen that ever I saw yet! If you can shoot as well with the long bow as you can make play with a sword, you shall come with me now to the greenwood. For I am no Reynold Greenleaf, nor yet no sheriff's man; I serve the best master that ever drew bow—his name is Robin Hood. What say you, jolly blade, shall we put up our swords now, and be off to Robin Hood?'

'With all my heart,' said the cook, 'for I think your master is better worth than mine! And we will not go empty handed, for the sheriff owes me more wages than he is ever like to pay.'

'And since he has paid me none as yet,' said Little John, 'and skimped my victuals too, we'll even help ourselves to what we can find.'

And they went to the sheriff's treasury, broke the locks, and helped themselves to three hundred pounds, together with a silver tankard to carry the money in.

'Ho, ho!' said Little John, 'now we are more than quits!'

And the two of them hurried off to the greenwood to find Robin Hood.

Robin was delighted to see Little John again, and asked him what news he had brought from Nottingham.

'Good news!' said Little John. 'The proud sheriff greets you well, and sends you his cook, his silver tankard, and three hundred pounds.'

'I dare wager,' laughed Robin, 'it was not by his goodwill these gifts came to me!'

'Now never mind, since they are come,' said Little John. 'And I've thought of a merry jest, dear master, if you'll wait here awhile.'

And leaving the cook and Robin to get acquainted, Little John ran off.

He ran and he ran, he ran five miles till he came to the place where the road to Nottingham passed by the borders of the forest, and there he waited. And he hadn't been waiting long, before he saw the sheriff come riding past on his way home.

'Why Reynold Greenleaf!' said the sheriff, 'what are you doing here?'

'Meeting you, sire,' said Little John, 'as a good servant should. But whilst I waited for you, I went into the forest, and I saw a most strange sight. I saw a splendid hart, sir, and he was coloured *green*! And with him were seven score of deer. And the hart's antlers were so huge and sharp that I dared not shoot lest he should slay me.'

'Coloured *green*!' said the sheriff. 'That is indeed a rarity. I should like to see that hart!'

'And so you shall, master, if you will come with me,' said Little John. 'But let your men go on their way home, lest so great a company should frighten that hart away.'

So the sheriff bade his men ride slowly on to Nottingham, and he and Little John set off through the greenwood. The sheriff rode, Little John ran, and when they had gone a mile or two, the sheriff began to feel nervous.

'Reynold Greenleaf,' said he, 'I think we had best turn back!'

But Little John answered, 'Whilst I have my good long bow in my hand, master, you need have no fear of man or beast.'

And he kept talking of the marvellous green hart. And the sheriff, not wishing to miss such a sight, rode on and on, till they came to the trysting tree; and there was Robin Hood with his merry men, just sitting down to supper.

'Lo, here is the master hart!' cried Little John. 'And here his seven score head of deer. And I think you'll agree that you never saw a finer hart in all your life!'

The sheriff swung his horse round: he would have galloped off, but Little John caught the horse by the bridle.

'Nay, nay, Sir Sheriff,' said he, 'my master, Robin Hood, would have you stay and sup with him.'

'Ah you wretched Reynold Greenleaf!' cried the sheriff. 'You have betrayed me!'

'And if I have,' said Little John, 'you have only yourself to thank. For when I was with you, I never got enough to eat. Neither enough dinner nor enough supper did I get all the time I served you. But now you shall learn how good men should be fed.'

'Come, sit down by me, Sheriff,' said Robin Hood, 'and eat and drink your fill—you will find, when you look in your

123

treasury, that your supper has been paid for. Now, make good cheer, Sir Sheriff! I promise you, by the love I bear to Little John, that your life is safe from me.'

Maybe so. But when the sheriff's own cook stepped up to him and offered him wine in his own silver tankard, the sheriff felt so full of woe that he could neither eat nor drink. He could only sit miserably there on the ground, watching Robin and his merry men as they emptied platter after platter. Yes, he was longing to be safe home again, was that woebegone sheriff.

But he was not to go home that night. By the time the meal was ended, it was growing dark, and Robin said, 'It's time you were abed, sheriff, and Little John shall be your chamberlain. Come, Little John, prepare your former master for the night, and see you do it properly!'

So Little John drew off the sheriff's hose and shoes, and his rich robes and his furred mantle. And there he stood in his shirt and his short breeches, looking very foolish. Then Little John wrapped him in a green cloak, and Robin bade him lie down and go to sleep. 'For this is our order, Sir Sheriff,' he said, 'under the greenwood tree.'

'Oh, oh,' groaned the sheriff, 'this is a harder order than any friar's or anchorite's. The ground is so hard, and my sides are so sore—how can I sleep?'

And Robin laughed. 'It's surprising how soon you'd get used to it, Sir Sheriff. I'm thinking it would be a grand thing for you to dwell with me here in the greenwood for the next twelve months. Then I would teach you to be an outlaw. It's a merry life, Sir Sheriff! See now, at supper you had no stomach for your food, though the meat was good and the wine also. But once I had taught you to shoot with the long bow and earn what you eat, I think you would not lack a hearty appetite.'

'Robin,' said the sheriff, 'rather than I should lie another night here, I pray you smite off my head! Yes, smite off my head, and I'll forgive you. For this torment I cannot endure!'

Robin laughed again. 'I wish you a good night, Sir Sheriff,' said he. 'For now I must sleep.'

So all night long the sheriff tossed and groaned, whilst Robin and his merry men lay peacefully sleeping, wrapped in their green cloaks.

In the morning Little John brought the sheriff his breakfast; but the sheriff pushed cup and plate away. He was all one ache, and his shirt and breeches were full of bits of twig and moss and withered leaves. He had his shirt off over his head, and was trying to shake it clean, when Robin came strolling up to him.

'And how do you find yourself this bright morning, proud sheriff?' said Robin.

'Robin Hood,' said the sheriff, 'for charity's sake, let me go home! And I promise you I will be your good friend for ever-more!'

'Have I your word for that?' said Robin.

'Indeed you have! Oh indeed you have! I swear it!' cried the sheriff.

'Then,' said Robin, 'we will come to an agreement.' And he drew his sword from its sheath and held it out to the sheriff.

'Now proud sheriff,' said he, 'you shall lay both your hands on my bright brand, and swear an oath to me.'

'I will swear anything, anything!' cried the sheriff, 'if you will only let me go home!'

And he laid his hands upon the sword.

'Now,' said Robin, 'repeat these words after me. "I swear, by this bright brand, that I will never plot to hurt good Robin Hood, but will remain his faithful friend for the rest of my life. And I swear that if I should meet with any of Robin Hood's merry men, in any place whatsoever, whether by day or by night, I will do them no harm, but help them in any way I can."'

The sheriff, with both his hands on the sword, repeated the oath, word for word after Robin. And then Robin put the sword back in its sheath, and called to Little John to bring the sheriff his clothes. And Little John, with a very grave face, dressed the sheriff again in his rich robes and his furred mantle, and his hose and shoes, and brought his horse and helped him up onto its back:

'So ends the service of Reynold Greenleaf,' said he with a deep bow. 'And I think Sir Sheriff, you will give your servant a good character, should ever he want one?'

The sheriff bit his lip and said nothing. Though sore and aching, and with his shirt and breeches full of leaves and prickles he set his horse at a gallop and was soon out of sight. But when he was sure that none of Robin's merry men could see him, he turned in the saddle, and shook his fist in their direction. He had no intention of keeping his oath.

Part 5. Robin Hood and the Monk

On the day that Sir Richard at the Lee was due to return to the trysting tree, that he might repay the four hundred pounds Robin Hood had lent him, he summoned a hundred of his retainers, clothed in white and red, and armed with bows and arrows, each arrow being four feet long, and notched with silver. And he set himself at the head of this gallant company, and rode off singing to the greenwood. Yes, he was going to visit Robin in grand style, as befitted a lord of lands to a lord of the forest.

And as he rode on his way, he came to an open space where a wrestling match was going on. A great crowd was gathered, and there were many competing wrestlers, for the prize was a splendid one: a fine horse, saddled and bridled, with gold ornaments on his harness; and in addition a pair of gloves, a gold ring, and a cask of wine.

And Sir Richard halted to watch the wrestling.

Now there was one wrestler who was superior to all the others, and no man could stand against him. At first the watching crowd cheered to see him win round after round, but by and by they grew angry; for the man was a yeoman stranger who came from goodness knows where, and each man in the crowd had his favourite on whom he had betted and hoped to see win. The cheers changed to abuse and curses, in which the defeated wrestlers joined: knives were pulled from pockets, bludgeons flourished, swords drawn. It threatened to go very ill with that champion wrestler, in fact he was in danger of his life, but Sir Richard, with a great shout, came to his rescue.

'Now by my faith,' shouted Sir Richard, 'and for the love I bear to Robin Hood, there shall no yeoman be ill-treated in my

126

presence!' And he charged the murderous crowd, followed closely by his hundred retainers.

The crowd scattered before the horses' hoofs, and the yeoman wrestler stood alone. Sir Richard stooped from the saddle and took him by the hand.

'This man has won the prize,' said he, 'and none shall take it from him! The fine horse, the gloves, the ring, and the cask of wine are fairly his! Up on your fine horse, my man, take the ring and the gloves and hie you home. But the cask of wine I will buy from you, and we will broach it here and now, so that these unmannerly knaves may drown their rage in a draught of good liquor.'

Then Sir Richard gave the yeoman wrestler five marks for the wine. The yeoman took the gloves and the ring, mounted his prize horse, and rode off to his home. And Sir Richard called his retainers together and continued his journey to Robin's trysting tree, leaving the crowd to make merry and recover their tempers over the cask of wine.

But all this had delayed Sir Richard. And under the trysting tree Robin was waiting. And it was long past dinner time.

'Master,' said Little John, 'do let us go to dinner!'

But Robin said no, he would not sit down to dine until Sir Richard sat down with him.

'But I fear Our Lady must be angry with me,' he said, ' since she doesn't send me my pay.'

(It was Our Lady, you will remember, whom Sir Richard had given as guarantee that he would repay his debt.)

'The day is not yet done, master,' said Little John. 'I swear Sir Richard is a true knight. He will come before dark, never you fear. But if I am not to dine, I must have some sport. I can't stay idling here with my stomach crying out for food!'

So Little John took his long bow and went off to seek adventure, and Much and Scarlet went with him. And when they came to the edge of the forest they saw a fat-cheeked monk riding along the highway. The monk was riding royally; he had fifty-two men with him, and seven heavily-laden pack-horses.

'Brothers,' said Little John to Much and Scarlet, 'though we are but three against fifty-three, we'll have that fat-cheeked monk to dine with us this day! Bend your bows now, and make all that company stand!'

So Little John and Much and Scarlet leaped from behind the trees and stood in the high road with their bows bent; and the monk and his company pulled up their horses in alarm.

'Sir Monk,' cried Little John, 'you must not go one step farther along the road. You have made our master very angry; he has been fasting these three hours for lack of your company.'

Now this monk was no other than the high cellarer of St Mary's Abbey—he who had chuckled over the idea of Sir Richard at the Lee's hanging himself. And besides being a greedy, heartless man, he was a coward. His fat cheeks were quivering with fear at the sight of Little John's bent bow. 'Wh-who is your master?' he stammered.

'Robin Hood,' said Little John.

And when they heard that dreaded name, all the monk's fifty-two men swung round their horses and galloped fast away. The monk would have followed them, but Little John had his horse by the bridle; and Scarlet and Much had jumped to seize the little page and the groom who led the pack-horses.

And so they brought them, monk, page, groom and pack-horses, back through the greenwood to Robin.

When Robin saw the monk he swept off his hood and bowed. But the monk was not so polite, he kept his hood on his head, and merely stared and shivered.

'Now by my faith!' said Little John, 'what a churl is this monk! Have off your hood, Sir Monk, before I strike it off for you!'

'Nay, let him be,' said Robin. 'Poor fellow, no one has taught him good manners. But surely, Sir Monk, you were not travelling alone?'

'Oh no, he had fifty-two men to bear him company,' laughed Little John, 'but most of them are gone.'

'Well, now we will summon *our* company,' said Robin, and he blew a blast on his horn. Immediately a hundred and forty of Robin's men came running; and each one, as he reached the place where Robin stood, took off his hood and went down on one knee.

'What is your will of us, master?'

'To entertain our gallant guest,' said Robin. 'Come, let the meal be spread, and you shall all dine with Sir Monk. Though, as for me, should I fast today and tomorrow also, I will not eat or drink until Sir Richard comes to share my dinner.'

So they brought the monk a bowl of water and a towel, and bid him wash his hands; and then they sat him on the green-sward, and Robin and Little John waited on him with meat and drink.

'Do gladly, Sir Monk!' said Robin.

'I-I thank you, sir,' said the monk. But though he was fat and greedy, he was never less inclined to enjoy his food than now. And he cast scowling glances at his page and his groom, who had sat down among Robin's merry men, and were eating and drinking heartily.

'Where is your abbey, Sir Monk?' said Robin.

'Sir, I am of St Mary's Abbey.'

'And what is your office?'

'Sir, I am high cellarer.'

'You are the more welcome to me,' said Robin, 'and you shall drink of our best wine. But I fear Our Lady Mary is angry with me, for she hasn't sent me my pay.'

'Master,' said Little John, 'Our Lady Mary has never failed you yet. I dare swear she has sent you your pay by this monk, for he is of her abbey.'

'Then if you have brought the money, Sir Monk, I pray you let me see it!' said Robin. 'For Our Lady Mary was to stand surety between myself and a knight, Sir Richard at the Lee, for a little money—four hundred pounds it was—that I lent him. And today is the day it should be paid back to me.'

'I swear to heaven,' cried the frightened monk, 'I don't know what you are talking about! I have never heard of Sir Richard at the Lee, or of his four hundred pounds, or why he borrowed it, or from whom he got it!'

'Monk,' said Robin gravely, 'I think you must be lying. For you said yourself that you are Our Lady's servant, dwelling in her abbey. Come, tell truth, are you not her messenger? And has she not sent you to me on the very day agreed on? I see your

129

pack-horses are heavy burdened. What money have you in your coffers?'

'Sir,' stammered the monk, 'but—but thir-thirty marks.'

So Robin sent Little John to look in the monk's coffers. 'And if he find but thirty marks, Sir Monk,' said he, 'I will not touch a penny of it. Nay, I will myself lend you some spending silver; for a monk of Our Lady's abbey should not go so ill supplied.'

But Little John came bounding back, carrying a heavy bag. 'Master, master,' he cried, 'Our Lady has been generous indeed. She had doubled the money you are owed. See, in this bag I have found eight hundred pounds!'

'Now by my faith,' said Robin, 'were I to seek the whole world through, I should never find a better surety than Our Lady has proved to be! Come, drink one more cup of wine, Sir Monk, before we part!'

But the frightened, sulky monk turned his head aside. 'It is scant courtesy,' he muttered, 'to bid a man to dinner and rob him of his money!'

'Well, well,' laughed Robin, 'it is our custom where we find much to leave but little.' And he bade his men bring round the monk's horse and the pack-animals.

'Now mount and begone, Sir Monk,' said he. 'Take my best greetings to your abbot, and bid him send me such a monk to dinner every day!'

Scarcely had the monk, with his page and his groom and his pack-horses, taken himself off, when a gallant company of riders came trotting down the forest glade: Sir Richard at the Lee and his hundred retainers. Sir Richard bade his men wait at a little distance, and he himself rode up to Robin, followed only by two servants who were carrying a present of long bows and arrows to give to Robin.

'God save you, Robin Hood!' cried Sir Richard, leaping from his horse and going down on his knee. 'God save you, and all your company! Forgive my being late. I came to a wrestling match on my way, and there I stopped to help a poor yeoman whom an angry crowd sought to ill use.'

'Sir Knight,' said Robin, 'I thank you for so doing. For whoever helps a good yeoman is my friend indeed! And have you now your lands again?'

'Yes, through your great kindness,' said Sir Richard. 'I have brought you here your four hundred pounds.'

But Robin wouldn't take the four hundred pounds. 'Our Lady has already sent me my pay,' he said. 'The high cellarer of her abbey brought it. But come, I have been fasting these many hours, and now you and I shall dine together. My merry men have already dined, for they are sad rascals, and in their hunger will wait for no man. But call up your followers, Sir Richard, and my men shall give them to eat and drink in plenty.'

So Robin's men served Sir Richard's men with meat and drink, and Robin and Sir Richard feasted and made merry together, and laughed over the monk's 'thirty marks' which had turned out to be eight hundred pounds. Sir Richard gave Robin his present of bows and arrows; and Robin insisted that they should share the monk's eight hundred pounds between them.

The moon was shining high above the forest that night before they parted. And as he turned to ride away, Sir Richard said, 'Farewell, good Robin Hood. In all the world there is no man that I love so well as I love you. And may I live to do you as great a service as you have done to me!'

Part 6. The Sheriff's Shooting Match

The Sheriff of Nottingham was an angry man. Ever since that miserable night he had spent with Robin in the greenwood he had been planning revenge. True, he had sworn a solemn oath never to harm Robin or any of his men, but that oath had been forced upon him: the sheriff didn't consider it binding—not he! Robin was an outlaw; to kill an outlaw—whether by trickery or by any other means—was a righteous deed. And the sheriff meant to have Robin Hood's life, however many lies he had to tell in the doing of it.

So the sheriff announced that he was going to hold a shooting match in Nottingham, and he invited all the best archers in the country to come and compete. The prize was to be an arrow, with gold head and feathers and a silver shaft. And the sheriff loudly declared that one of his own archers would carry away that prize, for there were no archers in the kingdom equal to them, he said.

'Ah ha!' thought the sheriff, rubbing his hands, 'that's the bait that will bring Robin Hood hastening to Nottingham! Robin prides himself that *he* is the best archer in all England, he won't endure to be placed second to any man!'

And the sheriff was right. As soon as Robin heard of the challenge, he decided to take it up. *What,* the sheriff to extol his miserable archers above Robin Hood! Bah! He would soon show the sheriff he was mistaken!

'And so, my merry men, we're away to Nottingham, to shoot at the butts,' said he.

'Not by counsel of me!' said Little John. 'The sheriff owes you a sore grudge, master.'

'We have his oath that he will do us no harm,' said Robin.

'Master,' said Little John, 'an oath on wicked man's lips, is a bubble easy to burst.'

But Little John couldn't dissuade Robin from going to Nottingham. All he could do was to make him promise to be cautious and not lose his life for want of keeping his wits about him.

So off they set on a merry May morning, with their good long bows slung at their shoulders, and their quivers full of feathered arrows at their belts.

When they got to Nottingham, they found a huge crowd gathered on the green where the butts were set up. The match had already begun; proud archers from all over the country were stepping up in turn to take their shots; from end to end of the green, townsfolk and country folk were jostling and elbowing to get a clear view of the contest, and the place echoed with the whang of arrows and the shouts and groans of the onlookers, as one archer hit the mark, or another missed.

The sheriff, in his best robes, and surrounded by a strong guard, stood at a safe distance from the target. But he was not really interested in the contest; his eyes were darting impatient glances, here, there, and everywhere through the crowd for sight of Robin Hood. Would Robin come? Was he going to fall into the trap? Or was he still skulking safely in the greenwood? If Robin did not come, the sheriff felt he would have gone to all this expense and trouble for nothing. What did it matter to him who gained the gold and silver arrow, if it did not prove the bait that should bring Robin to his death?

Ah! The sheriff clenched his hands, and his eyes kindled. There was Robin now, stepping boldly onto the green at the head of his men, the crowd falling back to let him pass, nudging each other and whispering, 'Robin Hood! See, Robin Hood!' And then, suddenly, such a wild cheering, such throwing up of hats, such shouts of welcome, that you might think it was not a miserable insulter of the king's officers and breaker of the king's laws, but the king himself who was stepping so proudly through that crowd of idiot onlookers! Little did they know, poor fools, what the sheriff had in mind!

'Master,' whispered Little John, 'look yonder. The sheriff's guards are strongly armed. I think that guard bodes us no good. Remember your promise to go cautiously.'

'And so I will go cautiously,' said Robin. 'And we will prove now whether the sheriff be a man of his word. There shall but six of us shoot at the butts: Little John, Much, Scarlet, Reynold, Gilbert, and myself the sixth. The rest shall keep watch, and stand in close array with good bows bent in case of treachery.'

And so it was quickly arranged, and the six of them took their turns at shooting. Whilst the arrows sped, the crowd stood breathless. When the arrows hit the mark, the applause that rose from that crowd was like the clamour of ocean waves on a stony beach. Surely never in the world was such archery as this! And though all six were good, Robin was ever the best. There was no doubt at all—the gold and silver arrow was his.

So, when all the shooting was done, the sheriff sent one of his men to summon Robin to him.

'Here is your prize, bold Robin Hood,' said he, holding out the arrow.

Robin went down on one knee and thanked the sheriff. Now he and his men would go back to the greenwood, he said.

'Not so fast, not so fast!' cried the sheriff. 'Outlaw and traitor,

Robin Hood, I arrest you in the king's name. Seize him, my men, bind him, make him fast!'

'Treason, treason!' shouted Robin, leaping back and drawing his sword. 'A fine way this, proud sheriff, to greet your guest! If I had you in the greenwood you should give me a better pledge than your lying word! To my aid, my merry men all!'

Robin had no need to call twice: a hail of arrows came flying across the green, and every arrow found its mark. The sheriff turned and fled, Robin was back among his men, shooting with the best of them, the sheriff's archers shot back, but they were no match for Robin's men: little by little they gave way, and followed their sheriff back into the town. As for the crowd of spectators, they had long ago taken to their heels, the green was all but deserted: but the town bells were ringing, the town horns were sounding, the sheriff was gathering the townsmen, calling on every loyal citizen to arm! arm! and capture Robin Hood.

And see, here they come, pouring out of the town: men-at-arms, archers, citizens, with swords and spears, with bows and arrows, with knives, with axes, with pitchforks, with any weapon they could snatch up. No sense for Robin now to stand his ground.

'Back to the greenwood, my merry men all! Back, back, before more slaughter's done!'

But what was this? Someone groaning at Robin's feet. Yes, there lay Little John, sorely wounded by an enemy arrow. Robin stoops over him. What is Little John saying?

'Master, master, if you love me, let never that proud sheriff boast that he has taken Little John alive! I beseech you, good master, draw your bright sword now, and give me my death wound. Oh master, dear master, now, now cut off my head!'

'Little John,' said Robin, 'that shall not be. We live and die together.'

And with the help of Much he lifted Little John up onto his back—a weight few men could bear—and set off at a staggering run, surrounded by his men.

It was a long way to the greenwood, and the town armed bands were coming behind them, thick and fast. Many a time Robin had to set Little John down, and stand to shoot back at the pursuers; then up with Little John onto his back once more, and away at a run: to stop and set his burden down again and yet again, and shoot and shoot and stagger on.

It looked as if it would soon have to be a pitched battle, for many of the town bands were mounted and were galloping on apace, when—a grateful sight for Robin and his men—a castle, double ditched and thickly walled about, loomed up boldly against the sky ahead of them. Once they could reach that castle they were safe, for it was the home of Sir Richard at the Lee.

One more stand, one more vicious rain of arrows, one more run: they were at the castle gates, and look—Sir Richard himself was standing there to urge them in. So through the open gates at a rush, and across the drawbridge: to hear the gates slammed and bolted behind them, the drawbridge hoisted, and Sir Richard shouting, 'Welcome, welcome Robin Hood and all your brave company! To arms, all you my servants, man the walls! Whilst I live none shall come in to injure Robin Hood, for of all men in the world I love him first and best!'

Yes, within those castle walls they were safe. The sheriff's mounted men, after galloping round the walls a few times, set spurs to their horses and galloped back to Nottingham: they could not face the hail of heavy stones that Sir Richard's men hurled down on them. Soon Robin and all his company were seated at table in Sir Richard's hall, eating and drinking heartily. Whilst Little John, having been carried up to bed, was having his wound washed and dressed by the gentle skilful hands of Sir Richard's wife herself.

Part 7. The Sheriff Complains to the King

Next day, the Sheriff of Nottingham sent out messengers to rouse the countryside and summon all good subjects of the king to arm themselves. And when he had assembled a large enough force, some on horseback, some afoot, he led them all off to surround Sir Richard's castle.

But the gates were fast, the drawbridge up, the castle well stocked with provisions: the sheriff might kick his heels out there for a month or more, for all Sir Richard cared. So the sheriff called on Sir Richard for a parley. Sir Richard came to stand on the battlements, and the sheriff, with a white flag clutched in his hand, shouted up at him.

'Traitor knight, do you understand that you are keeping here the king's enemies, against all law and right? Deliver them up and you shall go unharmed. Keep them, and I vow I will appeal to the king himself, and have your castle razed to the ground!'

And Sir Richard answered, 'Proud sheriff, what I have done, I have done with a clear conscience. But *your* conscience cannot be clear. You set a dastardly trap for Robin Hood and his men, and for that you should feel shame. I yield no man up to you until I know the will of our gracious lord the king. I have no more to say to you. Away with you to London; and when you bring me sealed orders from our king, I will parley with you again.'

Then Sir Richard went back into the castle, and the sheriff, in a fine rage, set off for London.

When he reached London, the sheriff craved an audience of the king, and bitterly complained both of Sir Richard at the Lee and of Robin Hood. 'They set you at naught, my liege!' he cried, 'they lord it over the north country as if they were kings themselves!' And he poured out a long story of all Robin's misdeeds, and of the knight's lawless aiding and abetting of him.

The king thought a while, and then he said, 'Go back to Nottingham, sheriff, and gather together as great a company of good archers as you can. And within this fortnight I will myself come to Nottingham. I will hear these two men speak in their own defence before I pass judgement on them.'

To tell the truth, the king was very curious to see this bold outlaw of whom he had heard so much. But the sheriff went back to Nottingham none too well pleased. And by the time he got back, Robin and his men were safely in the greenwood once more—the sheriff could not get at them.

Well, if the sheriff couldn't catch Robin Hood, at least he would do his best to get hold of Sir Richard at the Lee. And Sir Richard, who was awaiting the king's decision and suspecting no guile, had opened his castle again, and was living as usual. But the wily sheriff, with a strong band of armed men, was lying in ambush night and day to catch Sir Richard; and one morning, when Sir Richard was out hawking by the riverside, the sheriff and his men pounced on him, bound him hand and foot, and carried him off in triumph to Nottingham. The sheriff wasn't going to wait for the coming of the king, not he! He would hang up Sir Richard if it was the last thing he did in this life!

But the sheriff hadn't given a thought to Sir Richard's wife, who, as soon as she learned what had happened, jumped a-horseback and away with her at a gallop to the greenwood to seek out Robin Hood.

'A boon, a boon, good Robin!' she cried. 'Never let my wedded lord be shamefully slain. He is fast bound hand and foot, and is being carried to Nottingham to be hanged—and all for love of you!'

'Who has done this?' cried Robin.

'The proud sheriff and a company of his men,' said she. 'They are even now passing along the Nottingham road, some three miles on their way.'

'By heaven!' cried Robin, 'I swear this shall not be!'

And he blew three loud blasts on his horn.

Before ever the last echoes of the horn had died away, men came running to him from all sides, and Robin shouted, 'Haste, make ready, my men, bend your bows, see that your quivers are full! If any man lags behind now, that man shall live in the greenwood with me no longer! Away, away with us to Nottingham!'

And they set out at a run, more than seven score of them, leaping hedges, jumping ditches, taking every short cut. And when they reached Nottingham, there were the sheriff and his men, with Sir Richard bound among them, marching down the street.

'Stay, stay, proud sheriff!' cried Robin. 'Stay and speak with me. I would hear what news you bring from our lord the king! Never in seven years have I come so fast afoot; and I think my running bodes you no good, proud sheriff!'

And with that, Robin bent his bow. *Twang*, an arrow flew. The sheriff fell to the ground. He was dead.

Then Robin's men drew their swords and rushed upon the sheriff's men, whilst Robin sprang to Sir Richard at the Lee and cut the ropes that bound him. He thrust a bow into Sir Richard's hand, crying out, 'No horse for you today, Sir Richard! You must learn to run over hedge, over ditch, through mire, moss, and fen! You shall run with me to the greenwood, and there you shall stay with me, until I win a pardon for us both from Edward our gracious king!'

The sheriff's men, seeing their master lie dead, had little heart for a fight. Robin's merry men soon drove them off, and Sir Richard, Robin, and all his men, got safely back to the greenwood.

Part 8. The King and Robin Hood

A fortnight later King Edward arrived in Nottingham with a great company of knights. When he learned what had happened, the first thing he did was to seize the castle and all the lands belonging to Sir Richard at the Lee. He was so angry that he swore he would give both castle and lands, to have and to hold for ever more, to any man who would bring him Sir Richard's head.

But an old knight said, 'Ah, my liege lord, do not give Sir Richard's lands to any man whom you wish well. There is no man in this country may safely possess those lands whilst Robin Hood lives. It will be a head for a head, my liege. Give the lands to what man you will, before a day is come and gone, that man will lose his head.'

The king fretted and fumed; he would stick to his word, he said. But the days passed, and no one brought him Sir Richard's head; nor, though scouts were sent out in all directions, could any man bring the king tidings of Robin Hood, or of his men, or of Sir Richard. They seemed to have vanished from the face of the earth. But, in fact, they had only retreated deep, deep into the greenwood; and truth to tell, none of the king's scouts dared venture far enough to find them.

The king stayed six months in Nottingham; and at the end of those six months he was no nearer laying hands on Robin Hood than he had been the day he arrived. And the king became so angry that his knights scarcely dared venture near him. They were blockheads, they were scoundrels, they were cowards, they were weaklings! The king raged at them. *What*, had he brought them all the way from London, and not one of them had pluck enough, or gumption enough, to bring him within sight of those he sought?

And then one day there came a forester to the king and said, 'My lord and king, if you will deign to do as I advise, I can bring you to Robin Hood.'

'I will do anything to get a sight of that rascal!' cried the king. 'By heaven, I've a mind to give Sir Richard's lands and castle to anyone who can show me where Robin Hood is!'

'I am but a poor forester,' said the man. 'To serve my king is reward enough for me. But to do as I say, may not please you.'

'Leave me to judge of that,' said the king. 'What is it I must do?'

'Take five of your knights, my liege, and ride down to yonder abbey. Dress your five knights in monks' habits, and yourself put on the abbot's robes. Get you six stout steady-pacing horses such as monks ride, and a few pack-horses well laden, but not with gold. I myself will be your guide and lead you into the greenwood. And may I lose my head if you don't soon set eyes on Robin Hood!'

'By my faith,' said the king, 'a merry ruse! My hand on it, good forester, it shall be done!'

So the king and five chosen knights visited the abbey, got their disguises from the monks, and set out for the greenwood: the five knights in grey habits, the king dressed as an abbot, with a cowl, a huge hat, a richly-furred robe, and big, stiff boots. The king was in merry mood, he thought this a great adventure, and he sang as he rode along. Behind the five 'monks' followed a train of pack-horses, carrying bags well stuffed, but not with goods of much value; and before the procession rode the forester, to guide them on their way.

Well, they hadn't ridden more than a mile down through the forest glades, when from behind a tree out jumped Robin Hood, followed by Little John and Scarlet.

'Greetings to the greenwood, Sir Abbot!' cried Robin, laying his hand on the bridle of the king's horse. 'May I know to what abbey you are travelling?'

'To the Abbey of Westminster,' said the king.

'I wish you a safe journey thither,' said Robin. 'But the way is long, and by your leave, Sir Abbot, you shall stay and rest with us a while. We are yeomen of this forest, and we live by shooting the king's deer, for we have no other means. But you have churches and the rents from many a fair estate, and gold in plenty. Then give us some of your gold, Sir Abbot, for charity's sake!'

'As I live,' said the king, 'I carry no more than forty pounds with me. This fortnight I have been in Nottingham with his majesty the king, and all my gold has gone in entertaining his lords and knights. Forty pounds is all I have left. Take that, if it pleases you, good yeoman. And had I a hundred pounds, I swear I would not grudge to give you half. For I know that we who venture into the greenwood must abide by its customs.'

So Robin took the forty pounds, counted it out, and divided it into two equal portions. Twenty pounds he gave to Little John and Scarlet, who meanwhile had been rummaging through the pack-horses' saddle bags and finding nothing of value in them. The other twenty pounds Robin returned to the king.

'Sir,' said he, 'take this for your spending. Go on your way now without fear. We shall meet another day, when maybe your bags will hold something more worth the parting with.'

'I thank you,' said the king. 'But, good yeoman, may I know your name?'

'Robin Hood, at your service,' answered Robin with a bow.

'Ah, well met, well met!' cried the king. 'I have a message for Robin Hood from Edward our gracious king. He greets you heartily, and sends you his seal. He bids you come to Nottingham to dine with him.'

And from under his furred robe, the disguised king took out his royal seal, and showed it to Robin.

Robin fell on his knees. 'I love no man in all the world so well as I do my king!' he cried. 'Welcome to my king's seal, and welcome to you, Sir Abbot, for these tidings! I pray you now to come and dine with me!'

So the king got off his horse, and Robin took him by the hand, and led him to a wide grassy clearing among the trees. Little John led the king's horse, and Scarlet took the pack-horses in hand, and the five knights disguised as monks walked behind, leading their horses by the bridle.

'Seat yourself now, Sir Abbot, on this mossy bank,' said Robin, 'though more lowly than your chair of state, you will find it cushioned softly enough.'

The king, chuckling to himself, sat down. Robin put his horn to his lips and blew three loud blasts.

Immediately there came a rustling of leaves, a crackling of twigs underfoot, and the light sound of running feet. And out from among the trees leaped more than a hundred strong young men, all dressed in Lincoln green, all wearing swords at their belts, and all carrying long bows and quivers full of arrows. Not one glance did they give the disguised king, but each one, as he reached Robin, took off his green hood and went down on one knee.

'Saw you ever the like?' whispered the king to one of his knights. 'By my halidom, Robin Hood's men are more eager at his bidding than ever my men are at mine!'

The disguised knight was beginning to feel nervous. He didn't like the look of so many bold young men, so many strong bows and feathered arrows, so many bright swords. 'Were it not well to reveal yourself, my liege?' he whispered.

'All in good time,' chuckled the king. 'All in good time!'

In truth, the king was enjoying himself immensely.

'Now we will dine,' said Robin Hood.

And in no time, there on the greensward was spread one of Robin's famous dinners. The king was amazed as dish after dish was laid before him, with flagons of good red wine, and casks of ale.

'Make good cheer, Sir Abbot!' said Robin. 'And blessed may you be for your good tidings!' And he waited on the king himself, and so did Little John.

But Robin brought up one man and made him sit down on

141

the bank beside the king. The man was clothed in Lincoln green; he looked just like any other of Robin's merry men, but Robin treated him with such marked respect that the king asked who he was.

'Sir Abbot,' said Robin, 'he is the best friend ever man had. I owe him my life.'

'Nay, Sir Abbot,' said the man, 'it is I who owe Robin *my* life, for he saved me from the gallows.'

'This is a riddle I would fain solve,' said the king. 'May I ask your name, good fellow?'

'Sir Abbot, I am Sir Richard at the Lee whom the sheriff took and would have hanged.'

'Sir Abbot,' said Robin, 'he is Sir Richard at the Lee who gave me refuge when the sheriff would have slain me.'

The king frowned: then he laughed. So this was the man whose head he had demanded! Well, he was not sure now that he wanted that head, for as he sat there feasting in the greenwood all his ideas of right and wrong seemed to be getting mixed up.

When the king had feasted till he could eat no more, Robin said, 'Now, Sir Abbot, you shall see the sort of life we lead here under the trees of the greenwood, that you may give a true report of us to our gracious king when you meet him again in London. We will show you how we play our favourite game, which goes by the name of *pluck-buffet*.'

Then up jumped all Robin's merry men, took their bows in hand and saw that their quivers were full. The five 'monks' shrank back in fear, and even the king himself was startled.

'My liege,' whispered one of the "monks", 'I think it's time we were gone!'

'Tut!' said the king. 'Get you gone, if you wish. But I think it's safer to stay! A runaway might get an arrow in his back, you know. As for me, I have a mind to watch this *pluck-buffet*.'

See, now they are putting up two willow poles, one to shoot at, one to stand by.

'But Robin Hood,' cried the king, 'surely these willow wands are too far apart by at least a hundred and fifty feet!'

'Not so,' said Robin. 'They should be farther apart if the

142

glade were longer. This is our merry game, Sir Abbot. We shoot in turns, and he who misses the mark gets a buffet on his bare head from my clenched fist.'

'And may heaven preserve me from such a buffet!' chuckled the king, looking at Robin's brawny fist.

So they began to shoot. Mostly the men hit the willow wand, but sometimes they missed; and did one miss but by the fraction of an inch, that one ran to fetch his arrow, brought it to Robin, knelt, took off his hood, and received from Robin such a blow on his bare head as sent him sprawling.

'For this,' explained Robin, 'teaches us not to miss our mark. And now it is my turn.'

So Robin stood at the mark, bent his bow and shot. His arrow split the willow wand in two. They set up another wand. Robin shot again: again he split the wand.

'Such shooting as this I have never seen in all my life!' cried the king.

But Robin, cock-a-hoop with pride, would shoot again, and they set up yet a third mark.

Whang went Robin's arrow.

'Master,' said Little John, 'it is a true saying that pride goes before a fall! You have missed the mark by two fingers' breadth. And now you must stand forth and take your pay.'

'Since no better may be!' laughed Robin. And he fetched his arrow and held it out to the king. 'Sir Abbot, I pray you give me my pay.'

'Robin,' said the king, 'it goes against my order to smite a good yeoman! I fear I might punish you too severely.'

'Why man,' said Robin, 'smite on as hard as you can! I give you full leave.'

Then Robin took off his hood and knelt before the king. The king rolled up his furred sleeve, clenched his fist—and gave Robin such a buffet on the head as almost knocked him senseless and sent him rolling over and over on the ground, to the cheers and laughter of all his merry men.

'By heaven,' gasped Robin, getting to his feet, 'there is pith in that arm of yours, Sir Abbot! If you can shoot as well as you can strike, what are you doing lazing your life away in an abbey?

It were far better to dress you in a suit of green and join my merry men and me!'

'Truth, I am no abbot, Robin Hood,' said the king. 'But yet I fear it would not become me to join your merry men.' And he took off his great hat, threw back his cowl, and stood looking Robin straight in the eyes. 'Do you know my face now, Robin? Have you seen it pictured anywhere by chance? Or must I tell you who I am?'

'My king! My king!' gasped Robin, falling on his knees, as did all his men.

'Then mercy, mercy, Robin Hood,' laughed the king. 'Of your goodness and your grace, I pray you mercy for my five knights and me!'

'It is *I* who must ask mercy, my lord the king!' cried Robin. 'Mercy for myself and for all my men, and for my good friend Sir Richard at the Lee. For I have broken your laws this many a year, and my men, out of love for me, have done as I did.'

'Robin,' said the king, 'you shall have my pardon, on one condition: that you leave the greenwood and come home to my court, you and your men, to serve me loyally.'

Robin pondered for a moment, and then he said, 'Yes, I will come to your court and bring with me a hundred and fifty of my men, to serve you as best we may. But my liege lord, though I love you with all my heart, it may be that I shall not like your service. And then—'

'What then Robin Hood?' said the king.

'Why then I should have to come back to the greenwood and shoot your deer, as I have done before,' said Robin.

'Honestly spoken!' said the king. And he laughed again. 'Robin, I have a mind to play a trick on my sober subjects back in Nottingham. Have you any spare green coats to clothe my five knights and me?'

'Yes, in faith,' answered Robin. 'Both coats and hose and hoods in good plenty. I will clothe you this day, if you wish, as when I come to your court I trust you will clothe me.'

'Come then, my five knights,' said the king, 'we will be Robin's men for an hour or two, six outlaws of the best!'

Well well, a king who is young and in merry mood must have

his joke, and his knights must bow to his whim, however foolish
they may think it. So the five knights took off their monks' habits
and the king took off his abbot's robes, and in a trice there they
were, all six of them, clothed from head to foot in Lincoln green,
with longbows slung from their shoulders, and quivers full of
arrows at their belts. And the king jumped on his horse and
sang out, 'Six merry outlaws, and six merry outlaws, and six

merry outlaws we be! So hie and away to Nottingham and see the townsfolk flee!'

So off they all went, laughing and singing and shooting by the way. Robin and the king leading, and pausing often to play at *pluck-buffet*, for it seemed the king couldn't have enough of that rough game. And many a buffet the king got from Robin Hood, until at last he was crying for mercy.

'By heaven!' he cried. 'I should never be able to defeat you, Robin, though I shot the whole year through. But see, here we are at Nottingham town! And now for a lark!'

The people of Nottingham looked out. What did they see? A throng of men in Lincoln green galloping through the city gates. 'Oh, oh!' they cried, 'our king is slain, and here comes Robin Hood and all his company to take revenge on us!'

And old and young turned and fled, to seek the safety of their houses, and slam and bolt the doors.

And the king, as he and Robin and his merry men rode through the empty streets, laughed and laughed. But when they reached the market square the king said the joke had gone far enough, and he bid the outlaws raise a shout:

'Good people, your king is here! Your king bids you come into his presence!'

Then the people came out of their houses again: at first a few of the boldest, and then more and more, until the square was filled with a cheering, rejoicing crowd.

The king ordered a feast for one and all, with wine flowing freely; and after the townsfolk had eaten their fill, they lit bonfires and danced in the streets. And the king swore that this was the happiest day he had ever spent in his life.

He called Sir Richard at the Lee to him and gave him back his lands, bidding him jovially to be a good man for the rest of his life, and not to get mixed up with that sorry rascal Robin Hood again. 'Though the sorry rascal is now my faithful servant,' he said, 'and long may he remain so!'

And the next day, when the king returned to London, Robin and his merry men went with him.

But Robin's merry men were not happy at the king's court, and one after another they stole away and went back to the greenwood. So that by the end of a year Robin had but two of his men left with him: Scarlet and Little John. And those two only stayed because their love of Robin was so great that they would rather be miserable in his company than happy anywhere else.

Nor was Robin himself happy. And one day, as he and Little John were watching some young men practising archery, Robin gave a great sigh, and said,

'Little John, there was a time when I was known for the best archer in all England. And what am I now? A king's lackey! Alas, alas, if I stay here in the court any longer, I shall die of sorrow!'

'Then why stay, master?' said Little John. 'Why stay? Didn't you warn our lord the king that if you did not like his service you would go back to the greenwood?'

So then Robin went to the king and begged that he might go. But the king would only give him leave for seven days.

Well, seven days was better than nothing! And Robin and Little John and Scarlet set out gaily and travelled north, and on a bright morning found themselves back in the greenwood. The tree branches swayed and rustled above their heads, the ground was soft and springy under their tread, the birds sang, sunlight glanced among the green leaves, light and shadow made dancing patterns on the forest floor. Robin drew deep breaths of delight: the air was sweet—sweet!

And look, down the glade yonder, a herd of deer, running on slender feet from shade into sunlight, and into shade again. Robin took his bow in his hand: then he laid it by, smiled, and blew three loud blasts on his horn.

Look now! More pleasing to Robin's eyes than all the deer in the world, a hundred and forty-seven strong young men bounding towards him. A hundred and forty-seven strong young men, snatching off their caps and going down on one knee before him.

'Master, dear master, you have come back to us!'

'Yes, I have come back.'

'Never, never to leave us again!' they cried.

'I think—never to leave you again,' said Robin.

And he never did. Of course the king was vexed, but what could he do? Had he sent a whole army to the greenwood, he would never have caught Robin Hood alive. And this he knew full well. He soon got over his vexation. 'Robin Hood is a good fellow,' he said to his indignant lords. 'He shall do as he pleases. I shall always remember that he gave me the merriest hours that ever I spent in all my life.'

And Robin lived in the greenwood for the rest of his days.